"DON'T YOU WANT TO KNOW ABOUT MY DREAMS, MY FANTASIES?" JUD ASKED.

"Let me tell you what I dreamed about last night after you ran away from the pond."

"I really don't think that will be necessary," Cara replied.

"Oh, come now, any psychologist worth her salt is interested in her subject's dreams. In this case interpreting them won't be too difficult. Right before I went to bed, I was holding this lovely lady in my arms. I was so stirred by my desire for her—which incidentally was left unfulfilled—that my unconscious sought satisfaction in my dreams. Let me tell you . . ."

"Don't bother," she said sharply. She didn't want to hear about his dreams. He was talking about her, of course, and just knowing that he had dreamed about her was enough to make her head spin.

CANDLELIGHT ECSTASY ROMANCES®

TWICE THE LOVING

Megan Lane

A Candlelight Ecstasy Romance®

Published by
Dell Publishing Co., Inc.
1 Dag Hammarskjold Plaza
New York, New York 10017

Dell ® TM 681510, Dell Publishing Co., Inc.

Candlelight Ecstasy Romance®, 1,203,540, is a registered
trademark of Dell Publishing Co., Inc., New York, New York.

ISBN: 0-440-19148-3

Printed in the United States of America
First printing—March 1985

To Our Readers:

We have been delighted with your enthusiastic response to Candlelight Ecstasy Romances®, and we thank you for the interest you have shown in this exciting series.

In the upcoming months we will continue to present the distinctive sensuous love stories you have come to expect only from Ecstasy. We look forward to bringing you many more books from your favorite authors and also the very finest work from new authors of contemporary romantic fiction.

As always, we are striving to present the unique, absorbing love stories that you enjoy most—books that are more than ordinary romance. Your suggestions and comments are always welcome. Please write to us at the address below.

Sincerely,

The Editors
Candlelight Romances
1 Dag Hammarskjold Plaza
New York, New York 10017

CHAPTER ONE

Cara Stevens looked up from her paperwork, then brushed at her neat bun as Justin Garrett entered her office and firmly shut the door behind him. She watched as he easily covered the distance between the door and her paper-cluttered desk.

"Good afternoon, pretty lady," he said, smiling winningly at her, his dark brown eyes twinkling merrily. "Are you ready to delve deep into my subconscious and find out what a treasure I am? Or may I delve deep into yours and see if you care at all for me?" His drawl was slow, and he carefully enunciated his words. Cara loved to hear him talk.

"Oh, Justin, you know I like you," she replied casually, taking off her attractive glasses to more clearly reveal golden-flecked brown eyes fringed by thick, dusky lashes. "You're my favorite subject."

She laughed lightly, and while the laughter lingered, Justin bent near her. His long fingers spread out over her throat caressingly, and before Cara could move, he passionately claimed her mouth in a torrid kiss.

When Cara abruptly pulled away, Justin shook his head.

"I'd prefer to be your *only* subject," he said with an almost wistful sigh as he straightened.

Cara stared at the sculptured lips that had touched hers seconds ago. Justin was rushing her, in spite of the fact that she hadn't been very encouraging, and for the first time in years she was aware of the need to keep up her guard against a good-looking man's attractions.

She was here for research. Her work was her life; it didn't lie or cheat or hurt her. It was her first and only loyalty.

The thought briefly flooded her mind with a painful memory of Lance Madison, which she swiftly submerged. She didn't want to think about Lance; she didn't want to think about love. She had learned well that her brain was her best ally. And she had no intention of mixing work and play.

But she did find the man before her attractive. And she was flattered by his attentions. Although she was reasonably good-looking, she had discovered the hard way that there was always a prettier girl around the corner. Especially for a man like Lance—or Justin.

Anyway, she absolutely could not become involved with him. There had to be no chance of biased views in her study. She couldn't afford any complications that might arise from personal involvement.

"You know I can't write a book on twins with only one subject," she said.

He winked at her. "You could get a whole book out of me if you really tried."

"I'm sure I could," she readily conceded with a smile, "but my publisher has agreed to publish a book on *twins,* not *a* twin." As she gazed at him, watching while he settled himself on the edge of her desk, one long leg dangling, she found it hard to believe that there was a duplicate of this incredibly handsome man walking around.

For a moment her thoughts turned to Judson, Justin's elusive twin brother. She was eager to meet the man who was, from Justin's account, apparently the black sheep of the family, but she hadn't yet been successful. She wondered how easily she would be able to tell him from Justin if she should meet him.

Of course she had seen many twins who couldn't be differentiated on sight without name tags, but she hadn't previously encountered any so attractive. Her gaze wandered over Justin's appealing features. He was really special—intelligent, articulate, charismatic and very good-looking. She had no intention of becoming involved with him, but that didn't stop her from admiring his beauty. After all, she wasn't blind.

He was tall, over six feet, with straight black hair shorn in a precise and flattering cut, dark brown eyes with heavy black brows accenting them and an angular face that spoke of potent masculinity. Her gaze slid off the cleft in his rugged chin and settled momentarily on the broad chest hidden behind a light blue shirt and an expensive gray silk tie that matched the three-piece suit he wore.

It was summertime here in Virginia, but he looked as polished and cool as a gem. The air conditioning helped, of course, but she had never seen Justin look any way but bandbox perfect. He was an up-and-coming young lawyer of twenty-nine, and he knew about the power of appearances. He lived in a town of long-established practicing attorneys, but he was making inroads into their businesses, ironically without angering them, because of his charm.

He had charmed Cara, too, she told herself. She enjoyed his company; he had been a good friend, but she didn't want to go beyond friendship with this gorgeous man. The risks were too great. She was glad she would be leaving in a few weeks to return to her home in Costa Mesa, California.

It had been a long, long time since she had met a man who appealed to her so much. She didn't want to recall how long. Once again Lance surged unexpectedly into her mind. Lance Madison, *the* man in her past. He had taught her a painful lesson in love—one she was sure she would never forget.

She had forcefully put him into the far corners of her mind and then systematically buried his memory under an avalanche of knowledge. She was a little surprised that he should be surfacing now. Perhaps it was because Justin reminded her of him in many ways—the charm, the flattery—

and in his own way Lance had been as handsome as Justin. Tall and blond, with enchanting blue eyes and winning ways, Lance had stolen her heart.

No, she corrected. He hadn't stolen it; she had given it all too freely. What Lance had done was accept it and break it, crushing it carelessly in his wake as if it hadn't mattered at all.

Cara sighed. It had been years ago. After that she had devoted most of her time to her work. She had refused to dwell on her shattered love affair. Life did go on, and she told herself that she had been perfectly satisfied concentrating on her education and her research project. Until Justin began to shower her with his attentions.

She had known him three months and she had only been out with him a few times that weren't book-related. Not nearly enough to suit him, she knew, but more than she should have. She kept putting him off with explanations of deadlines and commitments, and though they were absolutely true, she knew that there was really more to it than that. She didn't want to get involved with any man.

She hadn't come to Virginia to find a lover, by any stretch of the imagination. As a fully accredited psychologist, she was here to write a book on twins, a topic that had absorbed her almost compulsively since she had roomed with an identical twin in college.

"How did you get involved with twins in the first place?" Justin asked, interrupting her thoughts as if reading her mind.

She smiled at him. "I've told you how already—a couple of times. Have you forgotten so soon?"

He winked at her. "I guess I wasn't paying attention, but don't be too hard on me. I can't think of anything but you when you're around."

How could she get angry with him when he flattered her so, Cara asked herself. "I'll tell you again," she said, eager to distract him from compliments she found too appealing.

"It started with an identical twin who roomed with me in college. She and her sister were attending separate colleges in different states, but they were tied to each other by some intriguing ESP, and, incredibly, they continued to behave as if the other twin were there."

She shook her head at the memory. "From telephone conversations they discovered that they often dressed the same on the same day, ate identical meals and engaged in many of the same activities. Most amazingly, at their respective colleges they met and fell in love with fraternal twins from their home state. If I hadn't seen it all for myself, I wouldn't have believed it," she said.

"I felt sure that it had to be more than coincidence," she continued, "so I set out to explore the subject. I kept gathering fascinating data on twins, researching and documenting every scrap of information I could find until I had reams of paper on the topic. Throughout college I did several papers, and I won some recognition for my research on the seemingly extrasensory twin relationship."

"And once you started seeing double, you just couldn't quit," Justin joked.

Cara smiled. That was just about what had happened. "I conceived the idea for a book, and fortunately my credibility opened the door for funding of the project by a pharmaceutical firm especially interested in schizophrenia."

It had been a dream come true, Cara reminded herself. She almost hadn't been able to believe it at the time. The firm had granted her extensive backing, and she had had the good fortune to pursue her passion worry-free. The timing had been especially good, for she hadn't yet gone into private practice and had no patients to be harmed by her absence.

For the past year she had traveled around the country studying twins in different regions. For weeks the South had been her focus, and finally she had settled here in Virginia to complete her research and her book.

11

She had rented an office downtown and gone to work each day to keep a routine and have a place where she only worked on her book. The small apartment she had chosen to live in was adequate, but hardly large enough to house all her book-related research materials and partially finished manuscript.

"Well, are you ready to go out to the ranch tomorrow?"

Justin's question brought her sharply back to the present. All month long she had been trying to set up an appointment with his twin brother, but Judson had remained obstinate about being interviewed. He had told her flatly and firmly that he would not agree, despite her pleas that it was in the interest of science.

Justin had warned her that his brother was impossible, and Judson's behavior certainly seemed to confirm it. He appeared to be as irascible and egotistical as Justin had said, and though Cara had made it a policy to judge no one by something someone else told her, she couldn't help but suspect that Justin's assessment of his brother was correct.

However, Judson's refusal to see her only made her more determined to interview him. Why was he so angry? What was he hiding? What was his relationship to Justin? *Was* he the black sheep of the family? And why?

But her persistence had been met with rude rebuttals and sharp refusals. Then, strangely, he had finally relented after her last call and invited both her and Justin out to the ranch —now that Cara's time here was almost at an end.

"Why do you think he suddenly agreed to meet me?" she asked thoughtfully. "Your brother—why did he relent? Do you know?"

A pensive look crossed Justin's face briefly; then he shrugged his broad shoulders. "I'm really not sure. Curiosity, perhaps. Maybe he's seen you on one of the local television shows, or out somewhere with me." He gave her his best smile. "You're going to be sorry he finally agreed. He's not a sweetheart like me."

Cara smiled. "Of that I have few doubts."

Her conversations with Judson had left little room for question, and she suspected that Justin's reasoning about why Judson had agreed was correct. Perhaps he had heard Justin talk about her and her research.

Justin had publicized it far and wide that she was writing a book on twins and that she was "researching" him for posterity. He had told absolutely everyone they met and had been helpful in getting her on local television and radio shows, thereby increasing the number of twins she could contact to interview.

Renting an office in the same building where Justin worked had been a stroke of pure good luck, and finding out that he was a twin had been more good luck. The luck had extended when he had helped her be accepted locally, but it hadn't gone far enough to include a meeting with his evasive brother.

Cara had thought surely she and Judson would meet somewhere at some time; after all, the town had a population of little more than forty thousand, and there were only so many places to go. At the least she had expected to meet Judson at a family gathering, but he had managed to absent himself from those.

"I'm ready to meet your brother," she said, looking into Justin's dark eyes. More than ready, she could have added.

"I'll pick you up at eight tomorrow morning. We'll eat breakfast out, then drive to the ranch. It's only about thirty minutes out of town, so it won't take long to get there. You don't need to pack anything fancy. Believe me," he said with a laugh, "Judson wouldn't know fancy if it hit him in the face. Slacks and tops—shorts if you wish—will be fine. And you might take along a pair of boots. Judson is sure to show you around his stables."

"I'll be ready," she said.

He stood up and walked around the desk. "Are we going out to dinner?"

Cara shook her head. "I have too much work to do. I'll be here for hours yet."

"Ah, Cara," he said, laughing lightly, "you know you'd rather be with me."

She couldn't deny that, but that was precisely why she had to keep working. "I'm sorry. I just don't have the time. There are so few weeks left before I submit the book."

Justin reached down, took her hands in his and drew her up. "If I can get away from the firm of Tate, Gibson, and Tate to ask you out to dinner, surely you can leave your work for two hours. My firm would like to see me with my nose to the grindstone constantly, too, but there has to be more to life."

"It's not the same thing. I'm working to meet a deadline. I can't take two hours."

"If you say so," he said resignedly, "but don't think you can keep putting me off." He leaned closer, his breath warm on her face, and whispered, "We'll have all weekend while you dissect Judson."

"Justin, you know this weekend is for work," she reminded him. She certainly didn't want him getting the wrong idea.

"Judson will have you running into my arms," he predicted. His voice sounded a bit strained as he declared, "My brother's a hard man."

Then he laughed deeply; Cara had a few seconds to wonder about his laughter before he lowered his head and took possession of her mouth again.

"Don't, Justin," she managed to murmur against his lips. She had absolutely no intention of giving in to his caresses. She was here on a research mission; nothing more, nothing less. She wasn't interested in discovering how easily a twin could break a woman's heart.

Reluctantly Justin freed her, and Cara stepped away from him. "I'd better let you get back to your work," she said firmly.

Justin's dark eyes were burning as if with fire, and Cara watched as his lips twitched slightly in irritation. Then the familiar smile lit his features.

"Ah, Cara," he said in a deep voice, "you're messing with my mind, don't you know? I hope I'm not just another victim of your charms."

She smiled at him; she knew her fear was more real than his. "That depends on what you have in mind," she said huskily. "I don't want to keep reiterating the fact that we are friends only and this is business."

His lips lightly brushed her cheek as he murmured, "We'll see what happens this weekend."

Cara was taken aback for a moment. This weekend. When she would be on an isolated ranch with Judson and Justin. She quickly recovered her composure. She could handle herself in any circumstances. She considered herself quite knowledgeable when it came to matters of the mind; after all, that was her area of expertise.

She was usually able to be objective and levelheaded, and she was sure she would be so in this case. Justin would go no further than she wanted him to. And that border had been established long ago, before she had ever heard of Justin Garrett.

"I'll see you in the morning," she said lightly, turning away from him. "Don't be late or I'll write it up in my book."

Justin laughed. "Oh, am I eager to see this book. I've never been a specimen for study before."

"I'll send all the participants a copy once it's published," she said playfully. "Until then you'll have to be left in the dark as to what I say about you. You'd better be on your best behavior."

Justin's warm smile danced across his lips; then he squeezed Cara's hand. She watched as he left, and when the door closed behind him her thoughts turned to the weekend. Mentally she went down the list of clothes in her closet. She had traveled light by necessity, but she sensed that this weekend was going to be very important to her.

She sat down at her desk and finished the notes she was compiling, then quickly gave some semblance of order to the debris scattered over the broad wooden surface. Having done that, she picked up her purse and went out.

When she had carefully locked the door behind her, she turned toward the most expensive shop in town. She would buy a new dress for her visit to the ranch. Judson might not know about fancy, but Justin did, and surely there would be at least one occasion for dressing. Besides, she hadn't dressed in far too long, and she was looking forward to an excuse to give herself a little extra attention.

Cara was packed and waiting when Justin drove up in his red Porsche the next morning. As she listened to him shutting off the strong sports car engine, a sudden and unexpected surge of excitement rose in her at the thought of meeting his difficult twin. She quickly assured herself it was because of the challenge he presented, but she couldn't deny that the man had already caught her interest with his hard voice and secretive ways.

She brushed a strand of sable hair from her face and chastised herself. Her behavior was indicating the strain of too many hours on the project, for never had she worn her emotions so close to the surface when she was working. She was a professional with several years of experience dealing with twins. There was no reason to see these two brothers as anything special just because they were so attractive and one was mysterious.

Because she had dressed in sedate black slacks and a sleeveless silver blouse, she had elected to soften the severe outfit by leaving her hair long and flowing. It swayed provocatively about her shoulders as she walked to the window of her second-floor apartment to gaze at Justin.

He pulled the key from the ignition, then dragged his long

length from the small car. Cara grinned as she watched him step out into the warm morning air. The day was going to be another scorcher, she knew, but Justin was predictably dressed in a lightweight summer suit. All that was missing this morning was his usual tie, and he looked quite dashing as he made his way up the walk.

Cara's landlady was already out, bustling around the yard tending to her flowers, and Cara listened as Justin effectively coaxed a hearty laugh from the old woman. The old cliché that he could charm the birds from the trees came to mind, and she smiled.

When he knocked on her door, she opened it to find him holding out a red rose to her. "Oh, Justin, you devil," she said with a smile, "you persuaded Mrs. Drexler to give that to you from the yard."

"Caught red-handed," he said, his eyes assessing her. His dark gaze roved appreciatively over her hair. "You look lovely like that," he said. "You're especially beautiful with your hair down."

Deciding that the best way to handle Justin was lightly, Cara playfully stuck the flower behind her ear and winked. Then she briskly picked up her small suitcase and held it out to him. She didn't want to begin the morning fighting off his advances.

"I'm ready when you are," she said too brightly.

Good-naturedly he took the proffered luggage in one hand and held out the other to her. "Any time."

Cara picked up her briefcase, slung her shoulder bag over her arm and slipped out the door ahead of him. When she had walked down the stairs with him, she saw Mrs. Drexler staring at them with open interest. "Good morning, Mrs. Drexler," she said.

The old woman nodded. "Morning," she said, but there was disapproval in her green eyes. She looked thoughtful for a moment, shrugged, then turned back to her plants.

Cara and Justin glanced at each other and smiled. The

17

generation gap was still alive and well, and when a couple
went off with suitcase in hand, there was nothing to do but
expect the worst. Never mind that Cara might have been
catching a plane or any number of other things.

As she slid into the car, Cara looked back at the old
woman, and she wondered what Mrs. Drexler would say if
she were told that Cara was going to spend the weekend
with the Garrett brothers on Judson's ranch. Somehow the
question unsettled her, and she fell silent as Justin eased the
car back onto the street and headed toward a café on the
outskirts of town.

They had eaten in the small café before, and Cara enjoyed
the atmosphere there. A jolly old woman with plump cheeks
ran the place, and everyone seemed to love her. She grinned
broadly when Justin walked in.

"Hello, Justin," she called out. "Take a booth and I'll be
right with you."

"Take your time, Mama Carson," he responded. "I'll wait
all day for you if I have to."

When the old woman's face glowed, Cara smiled. Justin
certainly had a way with women. But then she already knew
that, didn't she?

She spent much of breakfast studying Justin as he inter-
acted with the other patrons eating in the small café. Most of
them called him by name, some of the old farmers even
calling him Mr. Garrett, despite his protests.

Cara's face colored in embarrassment when the meal had
ended and Justin teasingly said, "If you're through taking
mental notes on me, we can go let you devote some time to
Judson."

"Was I that obvious?" she asked with a grimace. "I'm
sorry. I really don't see you like a bug in a jar." She smiled
and admitted, "It's just that you're the most delightful of the
twins I've had the pleasure to work with."

He grinned. "Flattery will get you everywhere. As long as

you think like that, you can be as obvious as you want with your scrutinizing."

Cara didn't want to sound frivolous. This was serious work she was doing, and she didn't want Justin to think otherwise. She should never have gotten even slightly personally involved with him. She hadn't anticipated it, and she never should have allowed it.

But after all, she reasoned, trying not to be too hard on herself, she was only human—and he was all too appealing. She liked him, and she knew so few other people in town. She had wanted his friendship, and the occasional times she had gone out with him had been her respite from an often grueling routine.

Her thoughts turned to Judson as she and Justin climbed into the car. At least she wouldn't have to worry about finding him too charming. His tone had told her all too well that at the most he would barely tolerate her brief intrusion into his life.

She ruefully realized that she was already forming a mental impression of him, and that was always a danger in her business. She had been trained never to do that, and she had always managed to be objective in the past. Judson, however, sounded unlike any of her previous subjects.

As they worked their way toward the ranch on winding back roads, Cara suddenly wondered if one of the reasons Judson didn't want to be interviewed was his reluctance to be compared to his brother. After all, it must be difficult to be a carbon copy of someone like Justin.

Glancing at him, she let her gaze skim his bold profile. He seemed to have it all—looks, personality, career—and what did the other brother have? Obviously he lived way out in the country and kept to himself. But why? Was he poor? Less attractive, less appealing than Justin, in spite of the fact that they were twins? Had he long ago found it impossible to compete?

The man intrigued her, and as they twisted farther and

farther back into the isolated hill country of Virginia, she told herself that he couldn't have much materially. As if to confirm her suspicions, the state-maintained road gave way to a gravel one, and even that seemed to wind endlessly on toward Judson's place.

Justin had grown curiously quiet as they drove, and though Cara didn't know why, she was reluctant to break the silence that had settled in the car. Outside the birds were chirping and summer insects hummed. An occasional cow mooed from a pasture, but an odd stillness had fallen on the occupants in the vehicle.

At last they crested a hill, then started down it. "That's Judson's spread," Justin commented laconically, and Cara drew in her breath.

"Judson's?" she repeated inanely. Justin hadn't prepared her for this, and she couldn't recall a time when she had guessed more incorrectly. Down in the valley below them a white fence wrapped its way around acres of beautiful land. Trees shaded a pond that glistened in the bright morning sun. A young colt kicked up its heels in frisky play.

In the center of all the beauty sat the most palatial home Cara had seen during her travels in the South. Colonial style, it sprawled across the lush grounds, stately and enchanting, a mansion far removed from the rest of the world. And Cara realized she could hardly wait to meet the lord of the manor.

Satisfaction wasn't long in coming. As though the sight of his brother's house had prompted a bizarre change in his character, Justin suddenly pressed his foot to the accelerator and shot down the gravel road to the one that led to the house. The roaring sports car hugged the road easily enough, and abruptly they arrived in front of Judson's home.

And there, standing on the columned porch, was the owner of the mansion. Sweet magnolia blossom, Cara thought inanely as she stared at him. He *did* look like the lord of the manor!

Cara's heart took on an inexplicably erratic beat as she stared at Justin's twin. He was the same height as his brother; he had the same dark eyes, the same heavy black brows, and the same masculine, angular face with a cleft in his chin, but beyond that he had blatantly tried his best to look different from his brother.

The jet black hair was as straight as Justin's, but Judson had let it grow longer and took no pains to keep it in the neat style that Justin wore. His skin was a shade darker than his brother's, bronzed by sun and wind. The skin around his eyes was lined, and deep grooves around his mouth suggested frequent laughter, though Cara found that hard to believe. He was dressed in scarred black boots, worn jeans and a western shirt that gaped at the neck to reveal thick, curling dark hair.

Cara fought against taking an instant and totally unprofessional dislike to him. He was raw and virile-looking, with an animal magnetism that no woman could miss, but everything about him cried macho male, from his arrogant stance to the challenge in his dark eyes.

"Well, here we are," Justin said, bringing the car to such a sudden stop that Cara had to brace herself with her hands against the dashboard.

She could feel the first signs of trouble making themselves evident. Justin had talked about his brother many times— calmly, rationally—but suddenly she was aware of the tension in him. When she looked at him she saw that his fingers were white where they clutched the steering wheel. What was it about his brother that brought out this reaction? Suddenly she wondered if she knew this man as well as she had thought.

She was not naive; she was aware that a subject could be less than honest in responding to questions, but she didn't believe that of Justin. Had she been blinded to logic because of her attraction to him? Only now did she recognize all the classic signs of twin rivalry; she hadn't even suspected it before with Justin.

She had seen other cases. She knew about the jealousy and the hostility that sometimes were part of the intense and complex relationship of people who were born identical, but she had a feeling this was going to be an experience out of her realm so far, an experience that would demand all her ability as a professional—and perhaps as a woman.

CHAPTER TWO

It wasn't until he strolled down the many steps to the car with a grace totally foreign to the image he presented that Cara realized she and Justin had been sitting like two dummies staring at Judson Garrett.

As Judson returned their frank gazes, he reminded himself that he was sick to death of being a twin, of having a double running around. Unfortunately it wasn't something one outgrew. He was a very private person. He didn't want people interested in him only because he looked just like another man—especially when the man was his brother Justin.

But this woman had been persistent and had sounded so sincere that he had weakened. He had always admired persistence in anyone; if something was worthwhile, then by God it was worth going after until you got it. And he had heard the rumors about the psychologist and Justin. Truthfully, he was just plain curious to know what she was like.

Now that he saw her he realized that the preconceived notion he had had of her was all wrong. His experience with women told him immediately that this one was trying to downplay her attractiveness, to hide behind her glasses and her profession. But even her windblown hair didn't detract from her good looks. He liked what he saw. She stirred some unnamed masculine emotion in him.

As Judson's brooding, dark eyes assessed her, Cara realized that she must look a mess. The brief, wild ride down the hill had caused her hair to whip madly about her face, and the rose she had put behind her ear was no doubt limp and loose in the aftermath of the wind and sun.

Just as she was assuring herself that she didn't care how she looked—after all, she certainly wasn't trying to impress this man—Judson reached out with a large, rough hand, and Cara jumped in anticipation of she knew not what. His ebony eyes holding her soft brown ones, Judson casually took the wilted rose from her hair. Then he grinned.

"Come on in and make yourself at home," he said in a wry, gravelly voice that was deeper than Justin's. Cara noticed that his words seemed to be directed at only her.

The sound of that rough voice unexpectedly played on her nerves. She had heard it before, of course, but combined with the rugged image of the man himself, it now had more impact. She made herself accept Judson's hand when he unexpectedly offered to assist her from the car.

"I'm Cara Stevens, the psychologist. Thank you for inviting me here to interview you for my book," she said as she felt his hard, callused fingers close firmly around her own.

"You're more than welcome," he said slowly in response to her introduction. "I think this will prove quite interesting."

"Do you?" she returned in the same lazy, suggestive manner he had used.

If that was the case, why had he refused so adamantly when she had proposed the interview weeks ago? Why agree now, when she had so little time and would have to rush wildly to include her study on him and Justin in her book? Or was he just being perverse? She was beginning to think he considered this interview a game. As she quickly removed her hand from Judson's, she felt a bright flush taint her skin, and although it could certainly be excused because of the heat, she wasn't at all sure that was the reason.

She drew in a deep breath and saw that her discomfort hadn't escaped Judson's keen dark eyes. He was still smiling at her in a way that made her acutely uncomfortable. It wasn't at all like her to lose her professional demeanor, but the sharp contrast between the two brothers startled her. She couldn't seem to stop comparing them physically. Judson was actually more handsome than Justin, though she hadn't thought that possible. But he was handsome in a way that didn't suit her; he had an aggressive, raw sex appeal that suggested he was a man of the earth, a man whose life was pared to the basics, a man not willing to devote time to the trappings of society. She doubted that he had any of Justin's intellectual ambitions or any of his charm.

She glanced back at Justin as he walked around the car, then lifted their suitcases off the luggage rack. He was scowling, something she had never seen him do before, and she wondered why he had agreed to come with her. She had requested it, of course, for she had wanted to see the two brothers together, but now she questioned whether it had been a good idea. It hadn't escaped Cara that the two brothers hadn't spoken a single word to each other so far. She wondered why Justin hadn't given her any indication of their strained relationship. In all the times that he had talked about Judson being difficult, never had he said that they weren't getting along.

With a brother on each side of her, Cara walked toward the house. She had interviewed many sets of twins in her years of study, but, unable to ignore the brooding silence, she felt extremely uncomfortable walking between these two handsome twin brothers, their six-foot height towering over her own five feet six inches. Cara could almost feel the hostility crackling between them. Surely they weren't going to spend the entire weekend without talking to each other. They wouldn't do that, would they?

How could she conduct her research if they did? She glanced at Justin when they reached the door, and she saw that his jaw was clenched tightly. When she looked at Jud-

25

son as he opened the door, she saw that he had seen her glance at Justin. A broad smile curved his mouth.

Damn him, she thought irritably. He was enjoying this! He had finally relented because he wanted to have a little fun with them. She sensed it, and she was sure she wasn't wrong. Apparently he had waited until she had established a relationship with Justin, then agreed to an interview. But why?

Sure that she would find out soon enough, she cautioned herself about getting angry. That wasn't the way to get the job done. Drawing in a steadying breath, she met his dark gaze.

"Thank you," she said cheerfully when he opened the door for her.

He nodded a little and smiled. Cara had the distinct feeling that he had read her mind and saw that she was trying to suppress her annoyance.

She was immediately assaulted by a sense of coming home as she gazed around the living room. It was the strangest sensation she had ever experienced, and that, too, unnerved her. Why should she feel so welcome in Judson Garrett's house? She didn't know a thing about this place—and darned little about the man, she now realized.

The room was expansive, and it was decorated with couches and chairs that were designed for comfort, despite their elegant appearance. A long oak coffee table and several end tables were laden with magazines and books, giving the room a homey, welcoming look.

Two walls were filled with bookcases that housed an assortment of books and other collectibles. A third wall was occupied by a fireplace surrounded by mirrored panels that reached the ceiling. The final wall was the backdrop for a grand piano. The colors used in the decor were calculated to nurture and relax—rich browns and tans, warm oranges and bright yellows.

No wonder she felt at home, Cara told herself. Anyone would. And besides, who would expect Judson's home to look like this? She realized that his rough-and-tumble appearance had caused her to anticipate very informal living quarters, despite the beauty of the colonial house, and if she had guessed that any musical instrument would be here, she would have thought of a guitar.

"Your room is this way."

Cara started when Judson spoke in a low voice near her ear. Her gaze darted to his, and she again saw that smile that had already begun to grate on her nerves.

"Thank you," she said coolly. She looked at Justin to see if he would follow, and she was surprised when a butler appeared and picked up his suitcase.

"Please show my brother to the third guest bedroom upstairs, Raleigh," Judson said.

When the man nodded, Judson started down the hall with Cara's suitcase in hand. Curiosity caused her to peek into each of the many rooms they passed en route—a study with more books, a formal dining room, a breakfast room, a spacious kitchen. The list went on, but when they passed a room done in black and silver, she knew without being told that it was the master bedroom of the house. She glimpsed a little of its massive beauty before Judson came to an abrupt halt at the room next door.

"That's mine," he said, indicating the room he had seen her look into. "I've put you here so you'll be close to me. For study and all," he added dryly.

"I see," Cara responded evenly. "And you've put Justin upstairs."

Judson's ebony eyes met her golden-brown ones. "Is there some reason why I shouldn't have?" He snapped his fingers before she could reply. "Yes, of course. You and he want to share a room. Now why didn't I think of that?" His dark eyes challenged her, and Cara was determined to remain cool.

"We do *not* want to share a room," she said emphatically. "It just seemed odd to me that you wanted to put so much distance between yourself and your brother and so little between you and me."

"You're prettier," Judson replied without expression.

The statement sounded like a compliment, but Cara wasn't at all sure it was meant to be. She was positive he had a motive for each and every action; however, she was still totally in the dark as to what it was. She reminded herself that she was schooled in patience; she would wait him out. Sooner or later he would show his hand.

He was standing there, watching her reaction, his broad frame blocking entry to the room. "Excuse me," she said, then tried to slip past him to enter.

To her dismay, he moved forward when she did and her body brushed against his hard chest, causing her nipples to tingle with unexpected sensation. Finding that she couldn't get past him and not wanting to continue touching him, she adjusted her glasses on her nose and stepped back. She was looking anywhere but at the man, yet she knew he was smiling at her.

"Sorry," he said. "I'm in the way, aren't I?"

Judson didn't know what it was about this woman that caused him to want to tease her. It was not in his nature to torment, but there was something so demure and poised about her, so serious and intent that it made him want to deal lightly with her to break through her professional persona to find out what she was really like. Despite his attraction to her, he didn't quite trust her. She was a psychologist trained to probe people's minds, and if she only wanted to play little mind games with him then she would find him a formidable opponent.

He paused meditatively. Was it only Justin that had made him agree to the interview? His reasons were elusive even to himself. He only knew that there was something about Cara Stevens that stirred his senses. And he found himself wondering if she was really involved with Justin, as the rumor mill had it. She didn't seem the type, but then who could say?

He stepped back so that she could enter the room. This is ridiculous, Cara thought. She didn't have to put up with his attitude—but she knew she would. Now that she had met Judson, he intrigued her even more than when she'd spoken to him over the phone. There was a story between these two twin brothers, and she wanted to hear it.

She reminded herself that she was here for research; she could put up with a little game playing if need be. In fact, once she had a feel for the man, she might even enjoy it. Two could play as well as one. And it might be quite revealing. Arms folded, she stood before him, waiting as he set her suitcase down. "You just make yourself right at home," he said. "When you've unpacked, I'll show you around the house and the grounds."

"Fine," she said. "I'll only be a minute."

"I never knew a woman who could say that and mean it," he said, his eyes laughing at her.

And have you known plenty of women, she wanted to ask, but she bit her tongue.

"Just come around to my room when you're ready," Judson said.

"I will." It took all her willpower not to respond tartly.

She waited until he had disappeared into his own room, then she made a quick study of hers. As with the rest of the house, it was beautifully decorated in neutral tones and expensive pieces of furniture. Cara found herself wondering where Judson had gotten all the money for this, but she was sure she would find out when she began to question him. There were lots of things about him she wanted to know. He was an enigma, and would make an excellent subject for study.

Had he been married? Was there a woman in his life now? She brushed impatiently at the thoughts. He would be asked the same questions everyone else was, and though personal questions were part of the survey, there was no reason for her to focus on them.

Determined not to take long in the room, she opened her suitcase, hung up her one good dress, then set the luggage in the closet. Anything else she needed to unpack, she would do later.

When she went to the next room she drew in her breath sharply. Judson's door was open and he was changing clothes. There was something primitive and very erotic about him standing there half-naked in the almost sinful black and silver decor of his room. A foolish image of the room as a glittering, beckoning silver and black spiderweb with Judson awaiting his next victim flashed into her mind, and she swiftly wiped it away.

He had stripped off his shirt and was reaching for another when his eyes met Cara's. She battled back the next thought that filled her mind: In his own rugged way he was beautiful, simply beautiful. Every muscle was outlined under his bronzed skin, and thick black hair covered his chest and trailed down to disappear under his jeans.

Of course she found him physically attractive, she reasoned; he looked like a rough cut of Justin, and she had never denied that Justin was handsome. But this was somehow a different kind of attraction.

She couldn't read the expression in his eyes, and she was determined that he wouldn't read the one in hers.

"Sorry," she said crisply, letting her gaze wander to the smooth black silk of the bedspread. "The door was open. I didn't know you were dressing."

"Well, I'll be damned," he murmured. "You did take only a minute." His eyes sparkled. "Just to show me that you could, right?"

She shook her head in denial. "I travel light. There wasn't very much for me to unpack."

"Oh?"

"I'll wait for you in my room," she offered.

"No need," he replied, pulling the shirt over his head and straightening the hem along his lean hips. "I'm ready. The other shirt was too warm."

Cara suddenly felt uncomfortably warm herself. "It is very hot today."

"Yes, it is, isn't it?" Judson's eyes held hers for a moment, then he deliberately let his gaze travel boldly over her figure. His eyes paused on her breasts, met her eyes again, then continued their leisurely trip down her hips and legs.

If he thought he could unnerve her this way, Cara meant to prove him wrong. But it wasn't an easy matter. She felt herself grow even warmer under the heat of his gaze.

Unexpectedly Judson gave her a hint of a grin. "This way," he said, moving out into the hall.

Grateful to be leaving his bedroom, Cara asked, "Is Justin going with us?"

Judson looked down at her. "We don't need him, do we? He's seen it all before. Take my word for it."

"No, we don't *need* him," she replied with just a trace of ire, "but you did invite both of us here, didn't you?"

She was acutely aware of his rude treatment of Justin, and she resented it terribly. She wouldn't have approved of that kind of behavior toward anyone.

"You aren't afraid to go with me alone, are you?" he challenged, his dark eyes glowing.

"Don't be ridiculous," Cara retorted.

"Then come on. I don't want him to come."

Cara could feel her blood pressure rising. She honestly wasn't sure which would give her the upper hand—insisting that Justin join them for the sake of being civil, or showing this cowboy that she was at ease alone with him. She chose the latter.

Taking his time, Judson explored the house and nearby grounds with her, although he said very little. The area was lush and lovely, and Cara gave her full attention to it. She was especially taken with the huge pond that glittered so

31

brilliantly in the hot sun. It was stream fed, and from where they stood, Cara could hear the water gurgling over the rocks in the sullen heat of the day.

"Do you ride?" he asked.

"No. It's one of those things I never got around to doing," she replied.

"You will," he said matter-of-factly. "I'll show you my horses. I've recently purchased half a dozen of the best brood mares money can buy. I intend to raise quarter horses."

For the first time since she had met him, Cara heard a hint of real emotion in this man's gravelly voice, and that emotion was pride. She had almost begun to think that he didn't feel—about anything.

"I also own part-interest in a horse that's making the race circuit out in your part of the country right now. I'm a limited partner, but I mean to get into this business all the way."

Cara smiled at him, happy to see him opening up to her, telling her about his plans and aspirations. But when he looked at her, he apparently decided that he had told her too much.

He fell silent for a moment, then added gruffly, "Anyway, I ride every day, and any guests I have usually like to."

"I certainly would," she said, wondering if he had many guests. He didn't seem the type, but it was still too soon for her to say.

It was almost noon before they returned to the house, but Cara realized that she had learned very little about Judson. She found herself comparing him to Justin again, and she wondered what the other, extroverted twin had been doing while they were away. She had been eager to talk with Justin, to ask why he hadn't leveled with her. And, oddly, she felt somehow as if she had betrayed him by going off alone with his brother. Yet she was here to interview Judson.

She had been amazed by her brief glimpse of Judson's

32

ambitions and his plans for the future, but she still hadn't found the door that would let her enter his life a little. And she didn't trust him. She didn't know if it was her instinct for self-preservation, but she knew she had to be on the alert at all times with him. She strongly suspected that he saw this weekend as entertainment.

"Where's Justin, Judson?" she asked, using his name for the first time.

"Jud," he corrected, and she found that she much preferred the shortened version. "I don't know where he is. Contrary to popular belief, I am not my brother's keeper."

When Cara gave him a displeased look, he said, "I'm sure he'll turn up for lunch. It's almost time, and he knows the way to the table."

"Which room is he in?" she asked as they entered the house.

An unreadable gleam glowed briefly in Jud's dark eyes. Then he pointed up the curved stairway. "Third bedroom on the left. You can't miss it."

Cara looked back at him once, then turned toward the stairs. She was halfway up before she remembered she hadn't thanked him for the tour. When she glanced down, she discovered him staring at her. "Thanks for showing me around," she said.

"My pleasure. I'm looking forward to seeing more of you." The hint of taunting was back in his voice, but Cara refused to acknowledge it as she turned away to continue up the stairs.

To her surprise, she found Justin stretched out on the bed reading a book. She rapped once, and he glanced up.

"Where have you been?" he asked. "I looked all over the house for you."

"I'm sorry. Jud took me on a tour of the house and showed me the grounds."

Justin sat up on the edge of the bed and ran his fingers through his thick black hair as Cara walked into the room.

33

"What's going on with you and him?" she asked softly.

When Justin didn't reply, she added, "I deserve to know."

For a moment he turned to gaze out the window; then he sighed heavily and met her questioning eyes once again. "I'm sorry. I really can't talk about it. It's very personal."

Cara sat down on the bed. She could see that he was deadly serious. He had no intention of telling her what the problem was, and although she didn't want to infringe on his privacy, she needed to know or else her study of this particular twin relationship would be worthless.

"You haven't dealt fairly with me, Justin," she said. "Why didn't you tell me about the breach between you and your brother? Why didn't you say something before we came here?"

For a long while he seemed lost somewhere in the past. Then he shrugged. "I never thought he would agree to an interview. I was positive he wouldn't have anything to do with anything involving me."

His eyes darkened as they searched her face. "I liked you from the first moment I saw you in the hall at the office building. The twin thing was just an angle I used to get to know you at first. I didn't really think you were serious about it, and I didn't think anything would come of our seeing each other."

He shrugged again and looked away. "When it did, I was already in over my head with you." He turned back to her, his eyes bright. "I'm crazy about you, Cara. I didn't lie about anything concerning me or my past or Judson. I just didn't deal with anything involving the last three years."

"Justin," she murmured, "I've told you how important my work is to me and that I don't intend to endanger my research because of personal complications."

"You've said that before," he replied, "but somehow I've never quite believed you."

Cara shook her head. "You should believe it. I'm not kidding. But I'm more concerned right now about what hap-

34

pened between you and your brother. We're friends. I want to help, but I can't do that unless you tell me what's wrong."

Justin's brooding gaze held hers. "It has nothing to do with you. It's not your problem."

"I'd like to make it my problem. Let me try to help. Anyway, I can't work very well if you two won't even speak to each other, and I can't help if I don't even know what you're quarreling about. You must realize that. You shouldn't have let me come here under the circumstances."

Justin was pensive for a short time, and Cara could almost feel his distress. He sighed raggedly, as if the weight of the world were on his shoulders.

"I'm sorry. I didn't know things would be this bad. I came here with you because I saw it as a chance to mend fences. I was wrong."

"What fences? What happened?"

All the light went out of his eyes. "I can't tell you that."

Now it was Cara's turn to look away. "Then I can't help," she said in a quiet voice.

An invisible wall sprang up between them, but before it could separate them, Justin started to speak in a monotone.

"Judson was always explosive. He got angry with me about something." He paused for a moment, then continued. "I tried to talk to him," he said tiredly, as if he had repeated it to himself too many times. "But he wouldn't listen. But then Judson never listened to anything he didn't want to hear," he added bitterly, his eyes burning with shadowed memories.

· Pained brown eyes met hers. "Frankly the nature of the incident was such that I'm just too embarrassed to talk about it. That's all I can say, except that time has only made it worse."

"I see," Cara murmured again. Clearly she wasn't going to gain any insight from Justin. And what about Jud? Would he tell her what had happened? Did *he* see this weekend as

35

an opportunity to mend fences? If so, why hadn't he made some attempt to initiate conversation with his brother?

She shook her mind free of the troublesome questions. Nothing would be gained by guessing. If she handled the situation skillfully the truth would come out eventually. And despite her misgivings, Cara began to see the situation as a psychologist's dream.

Here was a chance to explore the twin psyche *and* perhaps heal this bitter breach between the two brothers. She told herself that she had better be careful with Jud, but circumstances made her want to walk where angels feared to tread. Now that the hostility between them was out in the open, she could—and would—attempt to work with it.

Squeezing Justin's hand gently, she murmured, "There has to be a way to deal with this problem sensibly."

When a gravelly voice spoke from the doorway, Cara jumped. Damn, why was it that Jud had the power to set her nerves off like that, she asked herself. She really wasn't a jittery person.

"Lunch," he said laconically. He paused only long enough to look from Cara to Justin, then back again, before he turned on a boot heel and walked away.

Putting a pleasant smile on her lips, Cara said brightly, "Let's go eat, Justin."

"There's something about my brother that spoils my appetite," he replied grimly.

Cara suddenly felt very protective toward him. This really was an eye-opening experience. She hadn't noticed how vulnerable he was before.

"Hey," she said lightly, "don't let him get to you. That's just what he wants, and you know it. He did invite you here, so that's a good sign."

She wasn't at all sure about that, but she didn't want to let Justin know. She gazed into his dark, brooding eyes, and she wanted to see the familiar laughter there. If she could bring

36

these estranged brothers back together, she would consider it a greater accomplishment than finishing her book.

The twin relationship was a very special one, whether natural bonding actually occurred in the womb itself or whether, as some studies tried to prove, mothers caused their twins to become alike by treating them as one, making their clothing, hours, activities and environment always the same.

"Maybe I didn't know when I was well off," Justin said, interrupting Cara's thoughts.

She laughed aloud. She knew exactly what he meant.

Her laughter caused Justin to smile, then laugh, and soon the two of them were laughing merrily, their gaiety a much needed release from the tension they had been experiencing.

The laughter and smiles carried over as they went down to the formal dining room. Jud was already there, sitting at the head of the table, and Cara couldn't help but think how natural he looked—a Southern male presiding over his surroundings with some kind of innate superiority. That kind of macho mentality had never appealed to her, but oddly, Jud wasn't an unappealing sight.

To his credit, Jud managed a semblance of a smile when he saw them approach, but the smile had a quality that made Cara uncomfortable. Again she was aware of how good-looking and masculine the two tall, dark brothers were. It created in her a sensation unlike any she had ever felt when dealing with twins, but then, she told herself in all honesty, they were unlike any twins she had ever known.

Abruptly Jud stood and walked toward them. When he pulled out a chair for her, Cara fought to maintain her poise.

"Thank you," she said, barely glancing around at him. She was eager to penetrate his shell and hoped to gain some knowledge that would allow her to stand on some common ground with him.

When he had slid her chair closer to the table and started back toward his own, she asked, "Will it be convenient for

37

me to interview you after lunch? I have several standard questionnaires prepared, and I would like to begin my work."

She adjusted her glasses on her nose. That was quickly becoming a nervous habit she had acquired since meeting Jud, and she chastised herself for it.

His dark eyes met hers levelly. "I'm looking forward to it."

"Good." Cara had said it was good, but why did she have the feeling that he was looking forward to the session too much? Everything about the man made her uneasy, and she was more sorry than ever that she hadn't been able to meet with him much earlier in the summer, before she came to know Justin as well as she did.

She glanced across the table to where Justin had seated himself, then looked down the long length of the table. It would accommodate twelve, she saw, and she wondered why Jud had decided to have lunch here instead of at the smaller table in the breakfast room or out on the shaded patio. Had he had them sit here in the hope of intimidating them? Did he like the image of himself at the head of the table, presiding over the meal and his subordinates as if he really were the lord of the manor?

Lunch was an odd affair, with Justin talking nervously with Cara and Jud talking briefly with her about nothing in particular, but neither brother addressed the other. Several times Cara felt like standing and declaring that the whole scene was ridiculous.

But she didn't dare. Not until she got to know Jud a little better. She had a feeling that he was playing cat and mouse with her and Justin, but she wouldn't let him know she knew about his game. Not yet. Perhaps after lunch.

At last the unsettling meal was over. Coffee and dessert had been served, and Jud was leaning back in his chair, smoking a cigar. Cara told herself that that was just what she would expect from his kind of man; she disapproved of smoking for esthetic as well as health reasons, but strangely, as the moments dragged on, the pungent aroma of the tobacco began to appeal to her.

In all honesty, she found the sight of the cowboy and cigar a natural one. Somewhere in the far regions of her brain she noted that Justin didn't smoke and she knew he never had.

Finally Jud tapped the end of the cigar on the ashtray in front of him. "Are you ready to interview me now?" he asked, his eyes glowing as he looked at Cara.

She nodded, all too eager to get away from the strained atmosphere lunch had created. "I'll go get my briefcase."

"I'll go with you," Justin said, quickly sliding back his chair.

It wasn't Cara's imagination that Jud grinned tauntingly at his brother, and for a moment it took all her willpower not to demand to know why Justin had been invited here. She had a feeling she would need every bit of her control to deal with the interview with Jud.

When they had left the dining room, Justin turned to Cara. "I think I'll ask one of the stable hands to saddle a horse for me. I've got to do something. Lying around this house waiting for Jud to make his move is wearing on my nerves."

"Why don't you make the first move?" Cara suggested practically. "After all, someone has to."

Justin shook his head. "Oh, no. It won't be me. I was more than willing when I came here, but now that I see the way he's behaving, I'll let him play his game at his own speed."

"But you do know that's just what it is, don't you?" Cara asked, her eyes sympathetic. "A game?"

Justin nodded. "Don't worry about me. I can handle myself."

But Cara did worry about him. Being here with him in this situation was bringing out the maternal instincts in her, and she was caught off guard when he bent and kissed her mouth.

"See you later," he said, then he vanished up the steps.

Cara was still staring after him when she heard Jud's booted feet on the parquet floor. There was a brief moment of indecision when she didn't know whether to acknowledge him or not. Absurdly, she felt like she had been caught doing something naughty. Finally she forced herself to turn around and smile at him.

"I'll meet you in the library. That's it over there," he said brusquely. He pointed to a room across the hall, and Cara nodded. Then she quickly continued down the hall to her own room, her face flaming. She was actually embarrassed because she suspected that Jud had seen Justin kiss her. Why should she be? she asked herself. But she had no answer.

CHAPTER THREE

In her room Cara took enough time to compose herself again. She had to be in control. She was a psychologist, for goodness' sake. She knew about mind games and the people who played them. She couldn't let Jud throw her off balance.

That simply wouldn't do! She was going to earn her living working with people and their problems. She couldn't let some handsome man with a grudge against his brother disturb her. The problem here, she knew, was that Jud behaved as if she were the one who had a problem. It put her at a disadvantage, but she would soon change that.

She checked her briefcase to make sure she had the forms; the last thing she needed was to make a gaffe and appear incompetent. Taking time to freshen her makeup, she went into the bathroom off her room.

As she stared at her face in the mirror, she was startled by the overbright eyes and flushed cheeks. What was she letting that man do to her?

Her sable hair was still flowing loosely about her shoulders, and she decided that that wasn't the image she wanted at all for Jud. Quickly she tucked it into a discreet bun, jabbing the last pin in so hard it scraped her scalp. She allowed herself one more look, then took her briefcase in hand and went down to the library.

She rapped twice on the door, and when Jud opened it, she saw at once that she would have preferred conducting the interview in the dining room or the living room. The

41

library was much too cozy. Even the massive bookcases and long, dark wood desk didn't offset the feeling of intimacy in the room; it was smaller than the others, darker and very, very private.

Once Jud had closed the door, Cara felt as if she had been shut off from the rest of the world. She uneasily realized that it was exactly the effect he wanted.

Jud took her briefcase and laid it on a big round coffee table. "Sit down," he said, indicating the couch behind the table. "We'll work here."

He smiled for the first time when he said *work,* and Cara felt the hair on the back of her neck bristle. "This isn't a game, Jud," she said. "This is a very serious project, as I explained to you on the phone."

"Oh, I'm sure it is," he agreed all too readily, his black brows drawing together in a frown as though he was insulted that she had implied he thought otherwise.

Cara pursed her lips, sat down on the couch and began to take questionnaires and pencils out of her briefcase.

"A glass of white wine?" Jud asked, smiling at her.

A tray had been prepared with a decanter and two elegant wineglasses. "Yes, that would be very nice, thank you," Cara said.

Jud filled the two glasses, and when he had handed Cara one, he eased down on the couch beside her.

Cara couldn't help but think he was deliberately trying to invade her space, but nevertheless she calmly took a drink of her wine. When she had set the glass down, she picked up the first questionnaire and gave it to Jud.

"The directions are self-explanatory," she said. "If you have any questions, please tell me. Otherwise I'll leave you here to fill it out."

"Leave me by myself?" he murmured, his hypnotic eyes holding hers.

"Yes," she retorted dryly. "You look like a big boy to me."

He glanced at the questionnaire, then looked back at her. "I was never any good at this kind of thing," he said. "Why don't you read the questions to me?"

"I'm sure you can manage," she said evenly. "They're simple enough."

He smiled at her, then skimmed the long list of questions. "'Were you a bed-wetter as a child?'" he read aloud. Skipping down, he read another question. "'Do you bite your nails?'"

He began to read more and more of them, until Cara said firmly, "I know what's on the questionnaire. What we need here are your answers. You did agree to this, you know. No one forced you."

He looked over at her and made a *tsk*ing sound. "Cara," he asked, "do I detect impatience? Is that appropriate in a psychologist?"

It wasn't, and she had started to say so when he continued. "That is what you are, isn't it? A psychologist? Is that the excuse you give for running around prying into other people's lives?" He shook the questionnaire at her. "Or is this your way of getting your kicks?" He read another question off the list before she could reply. "How often do you have sex?"

His eyes met hers. "What gives you the right to do this? Who authorized this?" His tone was only half civil. This was the kind of thing that really got his goat, and he himself didn't know what had prompted him to agree to be analyzed like some creature under a magnifying glass.

Cara had to draw on every ounce of her strength to keep her temper. "No one had to authorize it. I'm writing a book. I am a fully accredited psychologist with funding from a major pharmaceutical firm for the project."

"Oh? And why did they grant you funding?"

"They're interested in schizophrenia and thought the twin tie might provide some relevant facts."

He looked at her skeptically.

"That's just a small part of the study. I'm particularly interested in the uncanny relationship between twins—the good possibility of being able to document extrasensory perception," she explained.

"To what end?" he said scoffingly.

"Tangible proof would be a godsend," she said fervently. "It would give credibility to police using mediums and clairvoyants to find the bodies of victims—and even the criminals who perpetrate such crimes. It would teach us more about mind control and the power to move physical objects with mental energy. It really does exist, I know it does, but society on the whole remains skeptical. We want a scientific explanation for everything."

"And the firm backing you? Are you going to sit there and try to tell me they want documentation of mind power?"

"Any study such as this offers some enlightening medical insight, too, and that's why the pharmaceutical firm is backing it."

"So that they can produce some new money-making drugs?" he challenged.

"We hope to learn something that will be useful in introducing helpful new drugs, yes!" she cried. "That's how we learn—and how we make medical and psychological advances. By research and study. Not just for twins, and not just for schizoid personalities, but for mankind in general."

He was still looking at her as if he couldn't believe what she had said. He clearly hadn't been impressed with her enthusiasm for ESP.

" 'How many times a week do you have sex?' " he repeated sarcastically. "What's that got to do with mind power or even schizophrenia? Or is this whole study based on the Freudian theory that everything is sexual? Have you already explored that side of my brother? Has he succeeded in getting you into his bed?"

Cara felt an angry blush rush up her cheeks, but before

she could formulate an answer that didn't betray her fury or the hostility she was experiencing, Jud continued.

"Well, don't be flattered. With your vast knowledge of the subject you have surely run across the dominant twin theory, and Justin must have told you *I'm* the firstborn—older than he is by seven minutes. Lucky seven! And he's spent a lifetime trying to make up for those minutes, trying to win everyone's love, to prove that he's my equal in everything. For him, with that simple mentality of his, that boils right down to the basics—sleep with as many women as you can."

Cara stared at him with wide eyes; he was surprisingly knowledgeable. Apparently he had studied his twin relationship with his brother in depth. But she was horrified by his callous dismissal of Justin's personality.

"Are you sleeping with my brother? I want to know."

Abruptly Jud was shocked into an embarrassed silence by his own outburst. Wasn't that what was at the heart of the matter—the question of whether she was sleeping with his brother? She interested him, but he wouldn't touch her if she was involved with Justin.

His question effectively interrupted Cara's speculation. "That's none of your business," she said tightly.

She felt like she was losing control now, and she would not allow it. He was the one doing the interviewing—and damned cleverly. He had no right to pry into *her* personal life. She knew he was transferring his anger from Justin to her, but she wouldn't give him the satisfaction of answering his questions. This leg of her research wasn't working out at all.

Abruptly she stood. "Coming here was clearly a mistake. I'm only interested in subjects who wish to participate in my research."

Jud stood up, too. "So you only want to include subjects who docilely let you pry and peep into their lives. Little twin boys and girls running around like matching pieces of a puz-

45

zle, telling you all about their lives and how they face the world together, two halves making a whole."

"I'm leaving. I don't like your attitude," she said, shoving the questionnaire back into her briefcase.

Unexpectedly Jud grasped her by her arms and spun her around to face him, causing her briefcase to fall and sending a shower of papers across the floor.

"But you want this, don't you?" he murmured, his mouth closing down possessively and skillfully on hers.

Cara was outraged. She couldn't believe what was happening. Just who the hell did this cowboy think he was? It was all she could do not to scream at him, but in the back of her mind she kept remembering a maxim one of her teachers had taught her: If someone can anger you, he can control you.

And she had no intention of letting this dominant twin control her. She decided she wouldn't lower herself to his level. Thinking he would let her go if she didn't dignify his assault by trying to fight him off, Cara let herself go limp and passive in his arms. But Jud wasn't easily deterred.

His mouth moved hotly against hers as his hands found their way into her hair to loosen it. Hairpins spilled down on the coffee table as her rich sable hair tumbled around her shoulders. Having accomplished that task, Jud let his firm fingers play along her neck and shoulders, barely concealed in the silver blouse. His body molded itself to hers, and she felt his hard warmth through her clothes.

When his tongue eased into her mouth, Cara turned her head, but Jud grasped her chin with long, hard fingers, making her accept his attentions. His mouth continued its forceful assault until, finally, he lifted his head and gazed into Cara's eyes.

Maxims be damned! Cara thought suddenly. Her thin thread of control snapped and she raised her hand and slapped his face before she knew what she was doing.

Jud stared at her assessingly. Then his lips formed a half-smile. "Isn't that what you really came for?" he murmured thickly. "With twins you get double everything—even twice the loving."

For a moment Cara was still too stunned to grasp the implication of his statement, and when she did, she fought to gain control of her temper. She occupied herself with bending to retrieve her papers.

Her voice was barely controlled when she spoke. "I see you can't resist the opportunity to insult your brother—and me. Is that why you invited us here? To satisfy your need to feel superior?"

It seemed that an eternity passed as Jud stared down at her. *Was* that why he had asked them here? Had he wanted to hurt Justin as he had been hurt? Was it because he had heard the rumors that Justin was involved with this woman? Had he wanted to insult her because she was attracted to his brother? Or was it because she wanted to pry into this particular part of his life? Was it all of these reasons, or some of them?

Had he invited them here out of curiosity, then found himself attracted to the woman? Wasn't that why he had kissed her? He had never expected her to be like she was—so cool and contained—and appealing.

He realized with a rush of anger that he *had* wanted to insult her because she was with Justin. But he had also wanted to touch her, to stir her from her apathy, to see if she had feelings behind that mask of formality and controlled superiority.

He could feel his face burning where she had struck him. Yes, she had feelings, and he had abused them. He was ashamed of himself for kissing her like that. She hadn't deserved his lack of respect. He had been out of line—way out of line.

She was right; he had agreed to the interview, and he had known what to expect—from the interview. It was the woman who had gotten him off the track. He had already told himself that she wasn't his type; she was too professional and reserved. He liked his women sexy and earthy.

But each time he looked at her, she both angered and moved him. He didn't need any more complications in his life—especially not any connected to Justin. And he had heard that she was his brother's woman.

That possibility made him burn inside, for he was attracted to her in a way he couldn't explain. She interested him as no other woman had in a long, long time.

Hell, he told himself disgustedly, this whole thing was a mistake, just like she had said. Already she had brought out the very worst in him, and now he was standing here like a fool wondering why he had behaved so badly, why he had touched her at all—why he had ever invited her here.

Still, when he looked at her he found himself wanting to get to know her, to sit down and talk with her without all that twin baloney. He wanted to tell her that he wasn't a man who needed to force himself on women.

Indeed, they usually came willingly enough. He wanted to explain his feelings to her and apologize. He wanted to start over with her, just the two of them meeting as any man and woman would for the first time. But there was the matter of Justin.

Why had she refused to tell him what her relationship was with his brother? He frowned as it occurred to him that she might be playing a game with him. But then he was the one who had initiated the dishonest play. She hadn't come here under any pretenses. She had said she wanted to interview him. She couldn't be held responsible for him wanting her.

Cara could feel his assessing eyes on her, but he did not speak. At last he reached down and grasped her upper arms. Then he slowly drew her toward him.

When she gazed up into his eyes, she found that she couldn't read the enigmatic expression there. He studied her face for a brief time, letting his dark eyes roam over each feature.

"Stay," he murmured at last. "Don't run off."

Cara searched his face. He hadn't apologized, and she found no indication of why he wanted her to stay. She shook her head. "I'd better go."

"Finish your research," he said.

"Why? What does it matter to you?" she asked coolly.

Jud's reply was softspoken. "I don't want to hamper advances in psychology or medicine. Stay in the interest of science."

She didn't know if he was mocking her or not, but she suspected that he had tried to use her in some way. Did he think she was involved with Justin and that he could get back at his brother by seducing her? Did he think she would have fallen into his arms that easily? Or did he think his appeal was such that no woman could resist?

"Stay," he coaxed again. "For Justin's sake. He wouldn't like to see you abandon his part of the study."

Cara's brown eyes smoldered with anger as she glared at the man before her. Once again she didn't know if he was being sarcastic or not, but it was almost as if he had issued a dare.

And there was Justin, she reminded herself. She did know that he wanted to mend his relationship with his brother, though only God knew why. Was she going to let Jud drive her away with one kiss?

She stared at him for a moment, trying to tell herself that she could get back on course. She could stay and do her research as she had planned. If ever she had encountered two twins worthy of study, it was Judson and Justin Garrett.

And if the truth be known, she was eager to get to the bottom of the rift between them. Now that she was calming down, she became more rational. Apparently Jud thought he had reason to hate his brother, and she wanted to know why.

Had he been hurt deeply? Was he a man covering his wounds with sarcasm and a show of macho strength?

Well, she was too good a psychologist to let one unpleasant incident send her packing. She lowered her eyes, wishing that her glasses were dark and tinted so that there would be no chance that Jud could read her expression. She didn't want him to know what she was thinking.

"Will you stay?" he asked more gently.

Cara had already made up her mind that she would. But she paused reflectively, playing for any discomfort she could create in Jud. Then she listened to her own cool voice, noting how distant and stern it sounded.

"I'll stay, but I want it understood that I'm here strictly to conduct research for my book. I won't tolerate any more manhandling."

As she heard herself say the words, she struggled with an unreasonable urge to smile. Manhandled. It was such an old-fashioned word, yet it was so appropriate for the situation.

Jud's dark gaze locked with hers, and just when she was sure he was going to tell her to take her forms and leave, he said, "Yes, ma'am."

Jud freed her, and she gazed after him as he walked to the coffee table and sat down. He picked up a questionnaire from the floor and began to fill it out. Cara vacillated briefly, then turned on her heel and left the library.

It wasn't until she was back in her own room, leaning against the door, that she realized how shaken she had been by Jud's touch. She could feel her skin tingling with the memory.

But the sensation was only temporary. He had embarrassed her, caught her off guard. That was why she was so disturbed by his advances. He had forced himself on her. It wouldn't happen again. She would make sure of that.

Since she knew it would take Jud some time to wade through all the questions on the form no matter how carelessly he answered them, for the better part of an hour she lay on the bed trying to block out her troubling thoughts. Eventually she felt restored enough to return to the library. She knocked on the door, then waited.

"Come on in," Jud called out. He had finished and was leaning back against the couch cushions, drinking a cup of coffee. "Have some?" he asked, holding up his cup.

"Yes, please." Cara was trying her best to behave as if she were relaxed, but it simply wasn't the case. Now that he had touched her, she was aware of him in a way she couldn't quite forget.

"Have you finished?" she asked as he poured her a cup of coffee.

"Yes, a few minutes ago."

"Oh, a speed reader?" she asked, thinking that he must have answered the questions in a slipshod manner.

He nodded. "Actually, yes. I don't have a lot of leisure because of all the work that goes with the ranch, so I took a class in speed reading." She could read nothing in his dark eyes. "I never could understand people who don't read broadly. I've gleaned a wealth of information from books."

I'll just bet you have, she thought to herself. If he truly did read widely, she had certainly underestimated him, in more ways than one. His attire had indicated nothing really, except probably the kind of business he was engaged in and his desire not to look like his brother.

"Obviously you had no problem with the questionnaire," she said. "That's good, because I have several more. I'll just leave them with you. I would appreciate it if you would complete them now. Then I'll have a chance to read them and tomorrow we can talk about relevant findings."

"Whatever you say." His tone was carefully neutral.

Cara could feel his gaze on her as she walked over to her briefcase and pulled out more questionnaires. She felt a heightened awareness of Jud, but she managed to appear confident and controlled as she handed them to him.

He reached out and took her hand in his. "I'm finding this very interesting," he said, staring up into her eyes.

Withdrawing her hand, Cara nodded unemotionally. "I'm glad. I suspect it takes quite a lot to interest you."

Those dark eyes whipped over her. "It depends on the subject matter."

"I think I'll go see if Justin is back," she said, ignoring her coffee. She would not engage in a verbal game with this man.

Jud was silent for only a moment. Then he said casually, "Why don't the two of you swim in the pool?"

She shook her head. "I didn't bring a suit, but that does sound like a wonderful idea."

"You don't need a suit," he murmured. "There's no one to see." He was driven by a need to know how intimate she had been with his brother, but pride forbade his asking again.

No one to see but Justin, Cara thought, but she kept her features carefully composed.

"I suppose so, but that really isn't my style. If I find Justin, we can just sit out by the pool. Better yet," she said, thinking of the shorts she had with her, "I can put on a pair of shorts and a shirt." She smiled. "What a marvelous idea. Thanks for the suggestion."

Without waiting for his response, she strolled back down the hall and up the stairs. Justin hadn't returned yet, but when she gazed out his window, she could see him coming toward the house, a hat in his hand. He seemed to be in a much better mood, and she went back down the stairs to meet him.

"Hello, pretty lady," he said cheerfully. "You should have gone with me. The ride was wonderful for the constitution and the disposition."

"I wish I had," she said. "I'm sure it would have been much more fun than—" She stopped abruptly. She had no intention of telling Justin about Jud.

"My brother must have given you a hard time," he said knowingly. "I told you he could be trying." He shook his head. "Oddly enough, he seems to have a way with women. Myself, I never could understand what the ladies saw in him."

Cara didn't even want to deal with that remark. "Well,

let's just say he can be difficult to get along with," she said casually. "But at least he's filling out the questionnaires. He suggested that we might want to swim."

"Now why didn't I think of that? I didn't bring a suit." Justin frowned. "A swim sounds heavenly after the ride in the heat."

"I didn't bring one either, but I'm going to slip into some shorts and a top. Did you bring shorts?"

"Yes. What a great idea." He started toward the stairs. "See you down here in three minutes."

"You've got a deal." Cara hurried back to her room and took a pair of white shorts out of her suitcase. She found a shirt that could be tied in a knot in front and quickly changed clothes. In minutes she was back at the bottom of the stairs, waiting for Justin.

It was several more minutes before he came down, and Cara's thoughts inevitably strayed to Jud in the library. She wondered what answers he was giving to the questions, but she would find out soon enough. After dinner she intended to go over them, making notes, comparing Jud's questionnaires with Justin's and documenting facts. It should prove quite revealing—but not as revealing, she suspected, as what she had already learned about the brothers.

Soon Justin came down dressed in only a pair of pale blue shorts, and as Cara looked at his handsome body, tall and muscled and covered with curling black hair, she wondered how Jud would look in such scant clothing—Jud with his detailed muscles and bronzed skin. She shook her head, trying to clear it of such thoughts and wondering why she should have them. She didn't even like the man. She could only attribute her active imagination to being overworked, and to the unusual situation in which she found herself this weekend.

Justin was grinning at her, and Cara felt a little self-conscious as his eyes ran over her.

"You have a very pretty body," he said, his voice a little husky.

Cara wondered if Jud could hear them, but in a house like this, that was ridiculous. He was down the hall, and anyway, what did it matter if he heard?

"Thank you," she said casually, not wanting to encourage Justin. Then she changed the subject. "Which way to the pool?"

When Justin held out his arm, she hesitated a moment, then locked hers in it. Arm in arm, they made their way down the hall and out through the breakfast room.

Jud had shown her the pool, but she hadn't known how to get there from inside the house. The house was laid out so that the pool was sheltered on two sides by a wing of rooms that opened out onto it.

Cara smiled as they stepped out into the humid heat. The water looked immensely inviting. Without giving Justin notice, she tossed her glasses on a lounge chair, loosened her hairpins, raced toward the water and plunged over the side.

When she surfaced she found Justin beside her, smiling affably. "I'll bet I can beat you in a race to the other end," he teased good-naturedly.

"I'll take that bet," she replied, stroking away from him.

Cara's expertise had never lain in sports, and Justin quickly surpassed her. As she watched him, she couldn't help but think how gorgeous he was as he stroked through the blue water. Then, to her chagrin, she was reminded of his identical brother. No matter how many times she scolded herself for it, she couldn't seem to stop comparing the two of them physically.

Justin reached the end of the pool first, but Cara had made a good showing and she wasn't far behind. Wanting to distract herself from her thoughts of Jud, she turned her attention back to Justin.

"This feels heavenly, doesn't it?" she asked.

"Mmm," he agreed, "wonderful. Especially after that

54

ride. And I need a little sun. That reminds me, there's a party in two weeks—a really big affair for this city. You will come with me, won't you?"

Cara pushed away from the pool edge, then treaded water with her hands and feet, trying to think of a tactful response. She didn't think it would be a good idea to see him socially. He was looking for personal involvement, and she wasn't.

"I don't think so, Justin," she said gently. "I'm under more pressure than ever to finish my book. Time has almost run out."

"Don't say no," he urged. "We won't stay long—three or four hours. The distraction will be good for you by then. Besides, the guests are your potential audience. They'll want to read the book because they've met you—and, of course, because I'll be in it. Come on, you owe me that much."

Cara laughed. She couldn't argue with his reasoning, but she knew she wanted to see him only as a friend. She sighed in resignation. There would be time enough to stress that again after they left Jud's house.

"I'll think about it," she replied.

Justin seemed content with her response, and for a while they swam together amicably. At last Justin climbed out of the pool. "I'm determined to get a little sun while I'm here. I spend too much time cooped up in that office."

Cara smiled. "I know exactly what you mean." Following suit, she made her way to the edge of the pool and Justin pulled her out. His hands lingered a little too long on hers, and to break the contact she turned away to pick up her glasses. Settling down on a lounge chair, she drew in a deep breath, then let it escape through her parted lips.

Neither of them had thought to bring towels, but they decided they would dry quickly enough in the hot sun. Cara adjusted her chair so that she was sitting up partially, then, dripping wet, she snuggled down on the pliable chair, stretched out her legs and closed her eyes. She could feel Justin looking at her, but she wanted to escape into her own little world. She pretended to be asleep, and it wasn't long before she was.

When she awakened, she was again aware of someone staring at her, but this time she sensed that it wasn't Justin. Her skin prickled. She could feel someone assessing her from the top of her head to the bottom of her feet, and she instinctively wanted to hide from that penetrating scrutiny.

She made herself open her eyes slowly. Judson was standing at the end of her chair, blocking the sun. He kept staring at her even when he saw that she was awake. Slowly he let his gaze travel the length of her body again before he spoke.

"You'd better go in and get ready for dinner," he said at last. "You've been out here too long. Somehow I don't think you can handle a lot of heat."

Cara was drenched with perspiration. The sun was beating down mercilessly from a four o'clock sky, but the heat she was really feeling was coming from the man standing in front of her.

"Thank you for your concern," she murmured hoarsely when she found her voice. "But I imagine I can handle a lot more than you expect."

"Really?" He raised one eyebrow questioningly, and Cara waited for further comment.

But it was not forthcoming. Jud lingered a moment longer, his gaze roving over her breasts and her bare midriff. Cara could feel her racing heartbeat, no matter how she tried to ignore his intimate appraisal.

At last he turned away without another word. Despite her unconcerned expression, Cara was grateful when he left. She raised herself on her elbows and glanced at Justin, still sleeping soundly in the enervating sun. She realized that they were both fortunate they already had tans, for otherwise they would have gotten burned by now. She looked back down at her shirt and sucked in her breath. No wonder Jud had stared at her for so long.

At some point the top two buttons had come undone, and

her breasts were spilling into the gaping vee. All that held it together was one button and the knot tied below her breasts. Her face flaming, she saw that the knot had only served to secure her bosom and push it upward so that it was more visible.

She glanced back in the direction in which Jud had disappeared. Then she quickly rebuttoned her shirt. When she was decent again, she reached out and touched Justin's arm.

Rousing sleepily, he tried to focus on her. "We'd better go in," she said. "Jud came out to tell us to get ready for dinner."

"How thrilling that must have been," Justin said caustically. "I'm sorry I missed it."

Cara managed a smile, but it was somewhat forced. She could still feel the way her body had responded to Jud's gaze. She was angry at herself for letting him affect her like that.

Abruptly she stood. "See you at dinner," she murmured, and then she, too, was gone.

CHAPTER FOUR

In the safety of her room Cara stripped off her damp clothes and headed for the shower. She could still feel the heat on her face, and it wasn't all from the sun. She had let Jud get to her, despite all her vows. He disturbed her in some way she couldn't quite rationalize.

A sudden memory of how he had implied that she had come here to find twice the loving rushed to her mind, further irritating her. The man was insolent and provocative, and it was all she could do to remind herself that there must be a solid reason for his behavior.

She dallied for a long time in the shower, letting the cool, refreshing water beat down on her body in full force. Eventually she shut off the taps and climbed out. She was drying herself on a thick towel when she heard the sounds of the shower in the adjoining bath—Jud's. She stood still, barely breathing. He was singing a song about undying love. Cara listened for a moment, faintly amused. He didn't seem the type to sing about love while he showered.

Then the smile faded from her mouth. Surely he knew that she could hear him. He was doing it deliberately, and she no longer found it amusing. He was making a game of this whole weekend, and she had no intention of being taken in by him. She turned back to her task and dried the rest of her body. Soon she heard Jud's voice fade as he finished his shower and stepped out. Abruptly Cara left her bathroom, suddenly finding it too intimate, knowing Jud was standing naked on the other side of the wall.

She decided to wear her new dress tonight. Taking it off the hanger, she held it up in front of her. It was made of a cool, filmy material in the palest shade of amber, and Cara knew that it would flatter her coloring. She lifted the full skirt and let it fall. It whispered against her nude body as it drifted back into semi-pleats.

The bodice was a pleated strip of cloth that was held up by a set of ribbons that went around the neck to be tied in back. There was another set at the waist where the cloth was the widest; the ribbons were long enough to wrap all the way around and tie in front.

Of course, Cara had no option but to go braless. As she stared at the garment, she told herself that she had been a bit too zealous when she bought it. On second sight, she wished it had more material. She could just imagine Jud's dark eyes roving over it—and her. The thought bothered her, but before she would let herself be influenced by Jud's possible reactions, she pulled on some lacy panties and slipped the dress over her head.

Spinning away from her reflection, she went to the bathroom and put on an apricot shade of lipstick that complemented the dress. She started to put her hair up, but the memory of Jud taking it down caused her fingers to halt midway to her head. She would leave it long. When she had put her glasses on, she returned to the closet to slip into two-inch-heel sandals. After giving herself one last glance in the mirror, she headed down the hall toward the dining room.

As she passed Jud's room she caught a glimpse of him in her peripheral vision. He was completing his own dressing. His shirt was still unbuttoned, and his bare chest muscles rippled as he slipped a belt through the loops of his pants. Cara told herself that he was deliberately leaving his door open, for whatever perverse reason, and though she was lured by the sight of him, she refused to engage in his game by turning back to look at him.

With her complexion heightened by the sun, and feeling pleased with her dress, she felt calm and sophisticatedly casual, and she was determined to keep her mind on business during dinner. Afterward she would retire to her room to read the questionnaires.

"Cara."

She was almost at the end of the hall, but she glanced back over her shoulder at the sound of the deep voice. Dressed in a pair of navy slacks and a pale blue shirt, Jud was more handsome than ever, and Cara found herself wondering why he had to be so good-looking and so impossible.

"Yes?"

"I'll walk with you. Did you get too much sun?"

"Pardon?" she murmured, glancing up at him. She had been too distracted to hear what he said.

"Did you lie outside too long? You were quite exposed—to the sun—for a long time." He let his gaze travel over her, from her hair to her shapely legs revealed beneath the swirling hem of her dress. His gaze eventually rested on the bodice of her dress, and she could feel her nipples tauten beneath his bold appraisal.

"Nice," he murmured. "Very nice."

Again Cara told herself that the dress was too daring, but then, she reminded herself, he had seen more of her earlier in the day—much more. And once again she was annoyed for letting him touch her vanity. She had no desire to be susceptible to his flattery.

"Thanks to you, I didn't get too much sun," she said, totally ignoring his compliment.

"Good."

There was an awkward pause as they made their way to their destination, and Cara saw, to her disappointment, that Justin hadn't arrived yet. She wanted to get on with dinner, get on with her assessment of the brothers. She wanted to find some answers for all the questions in her head concerning these two men.

"I finished the questionnaires," Jud told her as they sat down. "I left them in the library. You can pick them up after dinner."

"Thank you." For the life of her, Cara couldn't think of anything else to say. There were a hundred facts she wanted to know about this man, but she was going to let the questionnaires reveal them to her. She wouldn't give him the satisfaction of knowing how much he interested her. He was a paradox, and she didn't know quite what to make of him.

"Are you ready for that ride in the morning?"

She nodded, even though she had forgotten about it. "What time?"

"Right after breakfast, before it gets too hot and humid. We eat here at seven."

She nodded again, then added, "Good. I like to rise early."

His dark gaze held hers. "I'm glad to hear that. I'm a morning person, too." He grinned. "I can't think of anything I don't like to do better in the morning than at any other time."

Cara sensed that he had meant the remark to be suggestive, and she was determined that he wouldn't bait her. It was difficult to ignore him; he was raw and sexual and compelling, and she found herself looking all around the room to avoid him and his perceptive eyes.

As though he had read her thoughts, Jud continued. "Of course," he murmured, "as I'm sure you know, there are biological reasons behind that preference. For instance, a man's testosterone peaks at seven in the morning." His eyes met hers. "That's why making love in the early hours of the day is so much fun. It's also easier to make babies then, too."

Jud studied her to see the impact of his comment. She was a psychologist, but he would stake his life that she was a very vulnerable woman of little experience with men. She was too serious and too young to have gained much knowledge about the real world of men and women.

To his surprise, she handled herself rather well.

"So I've heard," she replied easily, refusing to let her gaze waver. But if he had intentionally made that remark to shock her, he had succeeded. She was surprised that she hadn't blushed, so unexpected and personal was the comment. And somehow, coming from him, it seemed even more provocative than it really was. She braced herself for more of the same, but Jud merely smiled at her.

Finally Justin entered the room, and Cara breathed a sigh of relief. He was dressed to the nines, as usual. Tonight he was wearing elegantly casual charcoal gray trousers, a pale pink shirt open at the neck and a white dinner jacket. But in spite of Justin's dapper outfit and the fact that the brothers were identical, Cara found Jud more handsome.

Thank God for air conditioning, she told herself. Without it Justin would roast in his dinner jacket. In fact, staring at him, she felt terribly underdressed, but then she was too warm anyway. She glanced at Jud. Maybe the room temperature itself wasn't all that hot. Maybe it was just that she was sitting across from such a virile, provocative man.

She forced the thought aside and gave Justin a bright smile. "We thought you'd never get here."

"I didn't think you would even miss me," he returned with a smile. He glanced at his brother, and when he saw that Jud's eyes were on Cara, his smile vanished.

The cook began serving, and an uneasy silence settled over the table. Everyone seemed preoccupied with the food, but in truth, Cara could hardly swallow her salad, and when capons were served, she only picked at hers. If either of the men sitting on each side of her noticed, he didn't comment. Jud's appetite was hearty, but Justin, too, only toyed with his food.

Cara was trying to think of some way to put the two men

back on friendly terms, but she wasn't sure how to accomplish it. The more she examined the situation, the more complex it became.

She had come here only to interview Jud, not to act in the capacity of family therapist. And yet that had become one of her major goals. Her mind was spinning with thoughts, but how could she begin the delicate mending process of healing wounds she didn't understand?

She decided to start at the beginning. With her best smile she turned to Jud. "Tell me, what is your favorite memory from your childhood?"

Jud seemed to digest the question; then he smiled at her reminiscently. "I suppose it would be the summer we spent down at an old swimming hole, swinging from vines that had wrapped themselves around an ancient oak tree. I guess we were about twelve then."

"We?" she murmured innocuously enough, although she was pleased he had used the term. "You and Justin?"

"Yes," he replied just as innocently. "I once had to rescue him from what he thought was a snake."

"If memory serves me correctly, I think it was the other way around," Justin said coolly.

"I'm sure you had a lot of fun when you were children," Cara interjected as smoothly as possible. When she received no answer from either man, she picked up her fork again and began to eat. Silence fell over the room once more. That strategy hadn't worked out too well, Cara told herself; she would have to try again later.

Eventually the meal came to an end and the three of them had an afterdinner drink. Justin had finally grown too warm and had slipped off his jacket. He was looking restive and anxious.

"I guess that wraps up dinner," Jud said. "I'll give you those forms." He was speaking to Cara, ignoring his brother. When he stood, he obviously expected her to go with him.

Justin stood, too. "Would you like to go for a walk,

Cara?" he asked, glancing briefly at his brother. "It's cooling off a little."

Although it sounded very tempting, Cara wanted to read the questionnaires Jud had completed. She hated to refuse Justin now, but she felt that she must.

"That sounds wonderful, Justin, but I need to do some work. Let's make it another time."

She couldn't miss the hurt expression in his eyes. He had wanted her to leave her business with Jud until later, but he knew she had come here to work.

"I'll see you later then, Cara."

"Yes." She watched as he walked away, and she felt sad for him. No matter what had happened between them, surely Jud could find it in his heart to forgive his brother, to take the second step in mending the break. After all, Justin had taken the first one by coming here.

Jud gallantly held out his hand, indicating that Cara should leave the room first, and she brushed past him, resenting his cavalier attitude and total disregard for his brother's feelings. She had gone halfway down the hall when she looked back at him. He was watching her walk, his gaze conspicuously on her legs.

"Did you encounter anything you couldn't answer?" she forced herself to ask, trying to strike up an impersonal conversation. Some of the questions on the surveys dealt with earliest memories, and many people said they simply couldn't recall such events.

Jud shook his head. "Only one or two."

Quickly turning back around, Cara entered the library. She tensed when Jud shut the door behind him. Surely he wasn't going to try to kiss her again. He wouldn't do that. Not after he had indicated that she should stay only to complete her research. But he merely reached for the forms and handed them to her.

"We'll talk about these tomorrow," she said. Then she

hurried to her room, hoping she held the key to the door of the brothers' discontent.

When she had slipped off her shoes, she settled down on the bed and eagerly began to study the forms. She was eager to learn about Jud—his past, his innermost thoughts, his ambitions.

And to her amazement, the man revealed in the questionnaires was nothing at all like the macho man she had thought him to be. She read on, fascinated by Jud's responses to her survey—his childhood, his personal habits, the women in his past, his sexual preferences.

"By God, he's a romantic," she murmured aloud, unaware that she had done it. "He's a deep, sensitive romantic."

She knew he wasn't lying; his responses were too automatic, too uniform, too consistent. His favorite composers were Chopin and Beethoven. His favorite painter was Renoir, his favorite painting was "The Dancer," and he loved the ballet.

But even more shocking to her was his sense of humor. She couldn't believe some of his responses to the questions.

To the question "What's your idea of an ideal mate?" he had responded, "A gorgeous woman who, adorned by nothing but a purple sash around her hips, the scent of violet on her skin, a rose in her teeth and a smile on her lips, will serve me a breakfast of eggs Portuguese, cream cheese, lox and toasted bagel, crisp waffle with fresh strawberries, fresh chicken livers sauté and a cocktail of orange juice, sliced strawberries, orange liqueur and champagne—in bed by seven A.M."

To the question "What's your idea of contentment?" he had answered, "Something warm and snuggly and cuddly, which will lie by my side, let me stroke it, pant for me and return my affection—not necessarily a puppy."

Cara laid the form aside for a moment, gently laughing aloud. Could this be the same man she had been spending time with, the man who persisted in taunting her and who behaved so coldly toward his brother? It hardly seemed possible.

She picked up the paper again, looking for clues to the resentment between the brothers, but, unfortunately, she found none. Now she wasn't sure what to think. Jud's answers had made her consider him in very different terms. He was as charming on paper as Justin was in real life—and much more sensitive, from all indications. His rough-diamond exterior had a highly polished interior.

For a long time she lay there pondering the two men, but coming up with no answers. When she really had a problem to solve, she liked to walk and think. For a moment she was sorry she hadn't told Justin that she would take that walk with him later this evening, but she realized she needed to walk alone to think.

Glancing at the clock, she saw that it was still early. She went to the closet and put on some sensible shoes, then walked down the hall and out into the night air. The evening sky was streaked with daring reds and pinks, and Cara strolled out under the descending darkness, her mind a thousand miles from the scenic beauty.

Instinctively she went toward the pond. She had seen it several times from her room, and though it was some distance away, she sought the peaceful atmosphere she sensed there. The evening was rich with sounds and smells. Birds sang contentedly, insects hummed and the blossoms of nearby plants filled the air with their fragrant scents. As Cara walked she began to relax a little, subconsciously soothed by her environment.

At last she reached her refuge, and beneath the graceful weeping willows ringing the pond, she sought peace of mind. In the serene atmosphere she tried to put her thoughts in some order.

She should simply conduct her interview and go home. The battle between the two brothers wasn't her problem. Yet the fact remained that she was concerned. She cared for Justin—and yes, she had no doubts that, given time, she could care for Jud, too.

There was something about him—something about the combination of virile primitive male and sensitive romantic man—that she found compelling. Not in a personal way, she quickly assured herself, but she felt she could now understand him as an individual a little better.

For a while she leaned against the sturdy, ancient trunk of a tree. Then, heedless of her new dress, she eased down onto the grassy earth below it. She could hear crickets singing out to each other, but she couldn't see them in the darkness that was beginning to cover the land.

The sounds of the pond lured her into contentment; smoothing the rough edges of her mind as the water bubbled and gurgled over the huge rocks along the stream bed. Its lullaby was so effective that Cara soon let go of her problem in her need to relax. Her total concentration was focused on the water as it crooned to her, whispering messages of calmness and peace.

She was startled when she heard faint steps coming her way, intruding on her solitude. She stood and grew more uneasy as she looked toward the house. A figure was approaching. She knew that Jud had a couple of men living on the premises to help with the horses, and it occurred to her that she had been foolish to come here alone without telling anyone.

The man came closer, and when Cara could barely make out the silhouette, she decided with immense relief that it was either Jud or Justin. But which one? Automatically she found herself praying that it would be Justin. But the gravelly voice that reached her ears told her in no uncertain terms that it was Jud.

"Cara?" he murmured. "Are you all right?"

She reached out blindly to pluck at the hanging branches of the willow, surprised by the concern in his voice. "Yes."

67

"What are you doing out here?"

"I wanted a breath of fresh air."

Jud laughed lightly. "The air in the house is fresher than this brooding, humid cloud."

"I wanted to get away for a little while," she murmured.

"From what? Were my answers to the questionnaires that bad?"

No, just the opposite, she could have told him, but she wasn't yet ready to discuss that with him. She hadn't settled the facts in her mind, and she hadn't compared Jud's answers to Justin's. She did know that she didn't want to be here with this man in the darkness at this pond far from the house.

"I wanted a little time to myself. You don't mind, do you?" she asked, trying to inject a little lightness into her voice and hoping he would take the hint and leave her to her privacy.

"Of course not," he replied. "I was concerned when I couldn't find you in the house. I didn't know what had happened to you."

"I'm sorry," she murmured. "It was rude. I didn't think you'd come looking for me. Let's go back to the house."

She tried to walk past him, but Jud reached out for her arm and drew her back to him.

"There's no hurry now. I know where you are." He had drawn her so near that she could feel his warm breath on her face. And she knew that was *too* near.

Pulling free of his strong fingers, she stepped backward. She tripped on a dead tree branch, and before she could fall, Jud caught her and held her to his chest.

Her full breasts tingled against the material of her dress. The barrier between her and Judson was so flimsy that she could feel the thick hair curling on his chest against the hardness of her nipples. His shirt was made of a very thin material, and it proved almost as useless as her dress in protecting her breasts.

"Did you hurt yourself?" he asked.

His voice was a soft caress in the darkness, and Cara felt her pulse begin to race. She almost expected him to lower his head and kiss her. The fragile moment seemed to stretch into eternity.

Then, abruptly, Justin's deep voice pierced the cloaking dark of the night.

"Cara! Cara! Are you out here?"

Cara really did not want Justin to find her here with Jud, no matter how innocent the circumstances were, after she had refused his offer to go for a walk. Already he seemed to think she was allying herself with his brother, and while that certainly wasn't true, she didn't feel like causing a scene. She suspected that was what would happen, no matter how she tried to explain.

As though sensing her indecision, Jud softly said, "Just be quiet for a moment, and he'll go away."

It seemed the easiest and most logical way to handle the situation at this point, so Cara did as he said, despite feeling guilty.

Justin called once more; then his footsteps faded.

"He's gone," Jud said.

Cara stepped away from him and ran her hands through her hair. "I'd better go, too," she said hurriedly.

"What's your rush?" he whispered, trying to pull her back to him. "Justin's gone. That's what you wanted, isn't it?"

Cara drew in her breath sharply. She hadn't wanted him to think that she was trying to get rid of Justin so that she could stay here with him, but it was so complicated she didn't know how to explain.

Before she could move away, she felt Jud's firm mouth on hers. For a brief moment she couldn't seem to decide on the right reaction. But the confusion lasted only a short time; then she turned her head and pushed at his shoulders.

"You promised you wouldn't do that," she said breathlessly. "I've explained to you that I'm here in a professional capacity."

"You're a woman as well as a professional," he told her in a low voice. "You can't deny that. I'm attracted to you, and you are to me. I sense it."

"You're wrong," she said vehemently. "Your ego won't let you believe that a woman couldn't be interested in you, but I'm not. My only concern is my research project. I am not attracted to you personally."

Before he could reply again, Cara had vanished into the darkness. For a short, unnerving time she thought that she was lost, but when she emerged beyond the perimeter of the trees, she saw lights glowing from the house. She headed through the darkness in that direction, her thoughts whirling.

She hadn't wanted Jud to kiss her, and she had no explanation for her unexpected confusion. After her bitter experience with Lance, she had wanted no other man's kisses. Jud was not at all like Lance, of course, but she sensed that he was a breed even more dangerous. She didn't need that kind of danger, and she didn't want it.

For some time Jud Garrett stared after the woman he had just held in his arms. He wished he weren't attracted to her. Yet he was. He hadn't intended to take her in his arms again, but she had been so alluring in the darkness, and he had sensed that she wanted him to.

Still, he didn't trust her. What kind of game was she playing with him and Justin? He didn't want to be anyone's fool, but he hadn't met a woman who appealed to him so much since Brenda. Brenda, he thought tiredly, and he lapsed momentarily into thoughts of the woman in his past.

Cara was breathless by the time she reached the house. Not wanting anyone to see her, especially Justin, she rushed down the hall to her room. She was grateful now that he was sleeping upstairs, but as she passed Jud's room, she shivered.

How she wished she weren't staying right next to him. She quickly stripped off her clothes, slipped into her nightgown and climbed into bed.

Jud's words kept echoing in her head. "I'm attracted to you and you are to me. I sense it."

And slowly, insidiously, her mind told her what she had not wanted to admit: Jud was right.

She was attracted to him in a way she had never been attracted to Justin. In Justin, she had found a handsome man whose company she enjoyed. But Jud stirred her senses in some very elemental way. She wanted to say it was only physical, but she knew that wasn't true.

From the first time she'd seen him, she'd found him intriguing, though she had wanted to dislike him for the way he presented himself and the way he treated Justin. And when she read his questionnaires, she found the man beneath the façade, the man all too easy to like.

What she had experienced in those few moments with him at the pond was powerful and intense. Not since Lance—

The thought of Lance sobered her. She wouldn't suffer that kind of pain again. She wouldn't be weak enough to let Jud entice her. She would do the job she had come here to do, then put him out of her mind.

She picked up the questionnaires Jud had filled out, wanting to study them further. She would forget what had happened at the pond and concentrate solely on her work here. Tackling the job with determination and mind control, she finally succumbed to her interest in the information before her.

So engrossed in her reading was she, so captivated by the subject, that she forgot where she was and why. Then sounds penetrated her meditation, and she looked around the room in dismay, realizing at last that she was still in Jud Garrett's palatial mansion.

She held her breath when she heard heavy footsteps in the hall, and she listened intently as they came closer and closer to her room. She knew it was Jud from the sound of the boots, but would he stop at his own room or would he come to hers? And what would she do if he did?

To her consternation, his footsteps stilled right outside her door. "Cara?" he murmured questioningly, and for once his voice sounded so much like Justin's that she couldn't be sure it wasn't.

She sat tensely in her bed and did not answer him. He didn't call her name again, but she sensed that he was still outside.

Eventually she heard him walk down the hall, enter his room and shut the door. And only then did she permit herself to breathe normally.

She could hear Jud moving about, apparently undressing, then showering. Finally the shower was shut off, and though Cara tried to concentrate on her work, she began to imagine what Jud would be doing next. Did he sleep in the nude? Did he read? Or did he turn the light out and fall asleep, untroubled by the kind of thoughts that teased her now?

She forced her attention back to the questionnaires, but for once her mind would not listen when she tried to assure herself that her interest in these twins was strictly professional. She knew there was more to it than that. She told herself that she should abandon the two brothers; she had enough twins for her book without them. But she couldn't make herself do it. She didn't want to leave them or this house. Foolhardy though she knew it was, she was caught up in some kind of emotional storm between the two men and she wanted to ride it out. Intuition told her that it would have a profound effect on her work, her life and theirs.

CHAPTER FIVE

A knock on Cara's door awakened her from fitful slumber. She roused sleepily and stared around the room, trying to get her bearings. The knock sounded more forcefully, and she murmured, "Yes?"

"Jud here. May I come in?"

If she hadn't still been half-asleep, she never would have been foolish enough to agree before she was out of bed and dressed.

"Yes," she murmured, regretting it as soon as she had said it.

Sliding up against the headboard, she drew the silk sheet up to cover her skimpy gown. And still when Jud entered the room, she felt exposed and naked.

His dark eyes whipped over her, from her tousled hair right down her sheet-enshrouded body to her toes, as though he had X-ray vision and could see every curve.

"It's six-thirty," he told her. "Breakfast is at seven, remember?"

She nodded, but she hadn't remembered at all. She was drained from last night and felt as if she could sleep a couple more hours.

"I'll be ready in a few minutes."

"Need any help?" he asked with a glint in his eye.

"No, thank you," she said crisply, wanting to blot out any remembrance of last night.

He smiled. "Then I'll see you in the dining room in a little bit. Don't forget to wear something appropriate for riding."

"I won't." But, in truth, she had forgotten all about riding today.

Jud glanced idly at the questionnaires on her night table. "Did the paperwork keep you up?" he asked, a lazy smile on his lips.

Before she could comment, he disappeared out the door. She stared after him. He had made no reference to last night, but then what had she expected him to say? She had made her position clear when she walked away from him.

But yet he had come to her door. What had he wanted to see her about? She bit her lip. Perhaps now she would never know, and surely it was all for the best.

Making herself get out of bed, she attempted to awaken fully. It wasn't easy, but a hot shower followed by a cold one helped, and soon she was dressed in slacks and a T-shirt top. She was thankful now that she had brought boots with her, and she pulled them on. After attending to her makeup, she plaited her hair in two braids and securely attached them at her nape with hairpins.

She had forgotten all about Justin until she entered the dining room. Both brothers were there, stiff and cold in the unnatural silence that shrouded the long table. Coffee had been served, and both pretended to be preoccupied with it.

When Justin glared at her, a flash of guilt washed over Cara. She remembered how he had called her last night as she stood in the dark at the pond with his brother.

"Good morning," she said quietly.

Justin's response was almost sullen. "I haven't seen much good about it yet."

Cara couldn't blame him for being cross. After all, his situation had only worsened since coming here. The breach between him and his brother hadn't been bridged at all, and surely it seemed to him that the woman he was pursuing was

74

more elusive than ever. Cara knew she would have to talk to him about that, but right now she couldn't face it.

Taking her regular chair, she waited tensely for the cook to bring her a cup of coffee. She needed something to fortify her for the day ahead. At last the motherly looking woman appeared, a smile on her face, her manner so cheerful that she must have been oblivious to the hostility permeating the air.

"Thank you," Cara said, wanting desperately to fill in the empty spaces with chatter.

"You're entirely welcome, dearie. Will you have grits this morning?"

Cara shook her head. "Just eggs and bacon, please."

"Fine."

The woman left, and the silence settled in again. "Are you riding with us this morning, Justin?" Cara asked, just to make conversation.

Justin shook his head. "No, I think I'll go off on my own." His eyes met hers hopefully. "Why don't you come with me?"

Jud looked at her, and, as usual, he directed his comments only to her. "You must ride with me this morning. Not to do so would be unforgivably rude, don't you think?" His smile was only half-teasing. "After all, I am the host."

Cara looked at Justin. "Come ride with us," she implored.

He looked from her to his brother. "No thanks."

Cara was at patience's end. "Justin," she cried, "you're behaving foolishly." She glared from him to Jud. "One of you has to break this ridiculous silence between you. You're brothers, for heaven's sake. Whatever has come between you in the past has to be forgotten and forgiven, and one of you has to make the first gesture of friendship."

Jud idly poured more cream into his coffee and stirred it with his spoon. Cara looked at Justin, her eyes asking him to make the first move if his brother was too bull-headed to do it, but she was met with cold ebony eyes. She had failed. She couldn't force them to reconcile, and all her talking was in vain.

Leaning back in her chair, she frowned in thought. She was a fool to think she could do anything to help, but she vowed she wouldn't give up yet. She saw this as a challenge, and her education surely had prepared her to handle it— somehow. Justin had taken the first step by coming here, she reasoned; she would try to get Jud to be generous in his attitude toward his twin. After all, he had invited him here.

But why? The question bothered her more than she wanted to admit, and she was glad when the cook set a big plate of eggs on the table. Bacon and hot biscuits soon followed, and the three people at the table made some show of enjoying the meal.

Justin was the first to excuse himself. "I'll see you later— if I can find you," he added pointedly, looking at Cara.

"I won't be hiding," she said. She knew he was referring to last night and she didn't mean that to happen again. This was her last day here, and she wouldn't regret the end of it one tiny little bit.

"Well," Jud said when his brother had gone, "that leaves the two of us, doesn't it?"

It does indeed, Cara told herself, and she didn't welcome the fact. She somehow likened it to being left in the middle of the ocean with no boat.

"Ready to go?" he asked.

She stood up. "As ready as I'll ever be."

Jud laughed. "Don't say it so enthusiastically," he joked. "What are you afraid of—riding or me?"

A slight smile curved her full lips. "Riding, of course. I've never had any dealings with a horse." Or a man like you, she wanted to add. She had thought she was out of her depth with Lance Madison, but he had nothing on Jud. In fact, he didn't even compare.

"There's nothing to it. I'll have you riding like a pro in no time," Jud assured her.

76

She didn't doubt it, and that was what bothered her. The more exposure she had to this man, the more she realized that he wasn't the bitter, reclusive man she had first thought him to be. He was capable, magnetic and totally in control. Which was more than she could say for herself at the moment.

When they had walked the considerable distance to the stables, Jud had a stable boy saddle a couple of horses. For himself he chose his regular mount, a spirited chestnut stallion, and for Cara he selected a docile mare. Even so, the animal didn't look docile enough. From Cara's position on the ground, the beast looked mammoth and threatening as she eyed her prospective rider suspiciously.

Jud walked over beside Cara and began to instruct her on the proper way to mount a horse. She reached for the saddle horn and tried to insert one foot into the stirrup and swing up as he had shown her, but to her chagrin, she failed miserably. Standing on the ground again, she adjusted her glasses on her nose nervously. She wasn't used to failing. All her life she had been successful at her endeavors.

Well, not all, she reminded herself painfully. There was always Lance to ruin her record, but she didn't count him when she could help it.

Jud grinned at her, and Cara felt like kicking him as he repeated the demonstration of the proper way to mount the animal. She tried again, determined to succeed, and this time Jud gave her an assist. She looked down at him when she was astride the horse, and she was acutely aware of the places where her body had touched his.

After easily swinging up in the saddle, Jud nudged his horse with his thighs and made a clicking sound with his tongue. Cara did her best to emulate him, but without success.

Jud laughed, and she found herself laughing with him. No matter how hard she nudged her horse, it stood still as a statue.

"Come on, Noble," Jud said, and abruptly he slapped the animal's rump.

Cara jerked backward when the beast unexpectedly launched into motion. Jud easily caught up with her and grasped the reins to slow the horse.

"Are you all right?" he asked.

"Just barely," she complained. "You almost caused me to get my neck broken."

His eyes were genuinely sympathetic, and Cara smiled. She hadn't been hurt, really; she had only been startled. "I'm fine," she told him, grinning wickedly.

He slapped her horse's rump, but this time more gently, and they set out across the flower-filled pastures to the barns that housed his brood mares. Cara bounced in the saddle more than she would have liked, but finally she managed to get the hang of it, and she found that she enjoyed riding immensely. It gave her such a feeling of freedom to fly across the land on the animal's back. Briefly she thought of Justin, and she was sorry he wasn't along, but she was too pleased by her own experience to linger on him for long.

When she and Jud reached the barns, he swung down off his horse and sauntered over to hers. Cara could feel her pulse racing faster with each step he took, and before he could reach up to her, she tried to swing her leg over the horse as she had seen him do in order to get down. She toppled to the side and would have pitched forward if he hadn't braced her.

He was grinning at her again, and Cara did her best to regain her composure as he put his hands around her waist and lifted her from the horse's back. He held her close to him, eye to eye for a moment, then deliberately eased her down the length of his body, a taunting smile on his lips.

After what seemed an eternity and must have been only mere seconds, Cara was on the ground. She wanted to say, Thank God, but of course she didn't. Stepping back from him, she said coolly, "Thank you. I almost fell."

"I know," he said with a grin. "It's your tendency to run away from me. You're going to get hurt if you keep that up —hurt bad."

Cara didn't know how much he knew about getting hurt, but she knew about it, and she had no intention of having it happen again.

"I can take care of myself," she said emphatically.

"I hope so," he murmured. "I hope so." Then he turned toward the barns. "Come on. Let me show you these beauties of mine."

Following at what she hoped was a safe distance, Cara walked to the fence. Immediately one of the mares came forward and nickered softly when she saw Jud.

He began to pet her, talking gently to her as he stroked her head. Cara was impressed by his sensitivity with the animal, and his patience. She realized that this was the man she had discovered in the questionnaires.

As long as the mare nuzzled Jud's hand and urged him to give her some attention, he did. She wasn't satisfied until Jud pulled a lump of sugar from his shirt pocket and fed it to her. Then he pointed out each of the other mares, telling Cara about them.

Cara knew nothing about horses, but it didn't take an authority to realize what beautiful animals they were or how content they were here on Jud's ranch. But then she could see how that would prove fulfilling for animal and man—or woman, she added unthinkingly. The thought startled her.

"This is a dream of mine finally come true," Jud commented as he gazed at the mares. "I sweated, worked and saved all the way through both high school and college to get the money I needed. Eventually my time and investments paid off."

"Handsomely," Cara agreed. "This place is very beautiful."

"Do you really like it?" he asked.

"Very much." She looked away in embarrassment without

79

quite knowing why. All the man had done was ask her a question.

She was glad when it was time to mount up again, and this time she was determined to succeed without Jud's help. It wasn't easy, but she did manage it, and it took all her control not to smile smugly at him. Some of her arrogance vanished when she looked at his face and saw him smiling at her. Still grinning, he tapped her horse's rear, nudged his mount, and they rode off.

They came to a section of land where two little boys were playing, and Jud halted both animals. The boys came racing toward him, and he climbed down from the horse to toss each of the children up in the air. It was then that Cara saw where his laugh lines came from. He was genuinely happy to see the boys, and he romped with them briefly before putting one on each horse.

The boy Jud set in front of her looked back and grinned sheepishly. Cara smiled, then watched Jud as he climbed up behind the other child. And she told herself that the man was beginning to display too many qualities that she admired.

He was warm and genuine with the children and the animals, and she found herself transposing W.C. Fields's old quote: A man who liked horses and children couldn't be all bad—even if he did hate his brother and cause a woman to lose her peace of mind.

"These are one of my ranch hand's children," Jud explained, scattering her thoughts. "That one is Raymond, and this one is Judson." He was unable to keep the pride out of his voice, and Cara was a little surprised to find one of the children named after him.

For one wicked, suspicious moment she wondered if there was more to this than met the eye, but when they had ridden back to the boys' house, she realized that the parents of the boy had named him after the boss out of respect and admiration.

Their mother was standing in the yard, watching them approach with a happy look on her face. "How are you today, Mr. Garrett?" she asked with a smile.

"Just fine, Libby, and you?"

"Couldn't be better," she replied. She shaded her eyes with her hand. "If you've come to see Raymond, he's still off at the north side of the fence where lightning sent the tree down."

Jud shook his head. "We came upon these little scoundrels and decided to give them a ride home," he said, looking at the boys with affection in his eyes. He swung down off his horse, then lifted little Judson down before he turned to take Raymond. When he reached his hands up to Cara, her heart started to pound. He put his long fingers around her waist and lowered her to the ground as easily as he had the children.

"Libby," he said, turning back to the other woman, "this is Cara Stevens." He grinned. "She's working on a book."

Libby nodded. "I heard about it the last time I was in town. You're a psychiatrist, aren't you?"

"Psychologist," Cara corrected with a warm smile.

"I believe Justin's told just about everybody he's ever met about your book," Libby said. "I can hardly wait to read it myself." She patted her son's head. "You know Judson's named after Mr. Garrett here. I always was fascinated with twins myself. I suppose most people are."

"Lots of them do seem to be," Cara said. She glanced at Jud and saw that the smile was gone from his full lips. It must have been the mention of Justin, she mused unhappily, his displeasure diminishing her own delight in the day.

"Cara and I are going out to the carnival on the Thomas Walden Orphanage grounds. We'd be happy to take the boys with us if you'd like."

"That would be real fine, Mr. Garrett," Libby said, grinning broadly, "but Raymond and I have already told them we'd take them ourselves tomorrow. Thank you for offering."

"My pleasure," he said. Then he turned back to Cara, who was still staring at him in amazement. He hadn't mentioned the carnival, much less asked if she wanted to go.

"Well, we'd better get back to the house," he said. Without further ado he swung up on his horse.

Cara was left to do the same, but not without some difficulty. She was determined not to turn to Jud for assistance, and finally she succeeded in climbing up on Noble's back. When Jud nudged his mount's sides, Cara did the same, but with much more vigor than she or the horse had anticipated. Noble bolted off through the grassland.

Jud caught up with them, and Cara rode at his side. "You didn't say anything about a carnival," she said. "You didn't ask if I wanted to go."

"Well, I thought you were here to get to know me," he said with a trace of sarcasm in his voice. "I want you to see me as a responsible citizen. I was sure you would want to go —in the interest of science and all. The children at the home are orphans, so once a year for a couple of hours I play father to them. You can't object to that."

"No, of course not," she murmured, at a loss to understand his sudden sarcasm as they rode back to the stables. Was it because Libby had mentioned Justin's name? Or was it the matter of the book that had annoyed Jud? She really didn't know.

At the stables she dismounted as he did, glad that she didn't have to rely on him to help her down. The stable boy took the horses, and she and Jud walked back to the house.

"You don't need to change," Jud said. "You look fine just as you are. It's a temporary carnival, of course, a traveling circus of sorts, but it's the highlight of the year for these kids."

"What a wonderful idea," Cara said. She thought it was

wonderful, too, that Jud participated, but she didn't say that. She sensed that it would make him uncomfortable.

She herself wanted to do some volunteer work with under-privileged children once she established her practice. She had always thought it was one of life's great tragedies that some children were abandoned, and felt unwanted so early in life. It created so many problems that haunted them all their lives. She was both pleased and impressed that Jud wanted to do something to help orphans.

"I would like to freshen up a little," she said. "And we should look for Justin so he can go with us."

"Justin really wouldn't be interested," he replied dryly.

"How do you know if you don't ask?" she retorted.

Jud turned on his heel. "You ask," he said over his shoulder, striding ahead of her. "I'll be ready to leave in ten minutes. I'll meet you on the porch."

Chagrined, Cara stared after him, wondering if there was no way to mend the tear in the brothers' relationship. If they never talked and if they refused to spend any time together, she didn't see how it would be possible.

Upset, she hurried after Jud, and when she had followed him inside, she went up to Justin's room. She was disappointed not to find him there. She made a quick search of the house, but she couldn't locate him. Having no idea where he could be, she unhappily abandoned the hunt. She had only five minutes left to clean up and meet Jud.

She was down on the porch ahead of him four minutes later. He looked at her mockingly when he joined her.

"What? No Justin? I told you he wouldn't be interested."

"I never found him to ask," she said tartly.

"But you looked, didn't you?"

"Yes, I did," she returned. "Quite hard, but he was no-where to be found."

She watched Jud's jaw muscle work convulsively as she walked beside him to his car, and she both regretted and resented his anger. She wanted to demand that he tell her what the quarrel was about with his brother, but she knew instinctively he would refuse—and probably get even angrier. She would wait until a more opportune time—if there ever was one.

The carnival was on the orphanage grounds, about twenty minutes from Jud's ranch. Neither Cara nor he spoke during the ride there, and Cara couldn't help but think the carnival was going to be a dismal affair under the present circumstances.

When they arrived, she gazed at the assortment of rides and game and food stands. The amusement center was just opening for the day, and she saw a short line of people waiting to buy tickets to enter.

"We'll go pick up our kids," Jud said.

Cara hadn't been quite sure how this was supposed to work, but to her pleasure, she and Jud went to the reception hall of the orphanage and waited until a little blond-haired girl about eight years old and two redheaded, freckle-faced boys of about ten and eleven came out. Although the children had been neatly groomed, one of the boys had a cowlick that caused a lock of his bright hair to stand up.

Cara was taken with him right away. She simply couldn't help herself. After they were all introduced, they set out across the grounds to the carnival, the children—Susie, Jim and Eddy—practically bursting with anticipation.

"You can ride anything you want, and you can eat anything within reason," Jud told them.

Cara smiled at him over their heads. The day was looking better.

Their first ride was the Ferris wheel, and Jud put the two boys in the car in front of them. Then he climbed in with Susie and Cara.

Despite the child between them, Cara was intensely aware of him as they went higher and higher into the air. She felt Jud's arm around her shoulder, his hand resting familiarly just above her breast. She glanced at him, but he didn't seem to be aware that he was touching her so intimately.

She debated whether she should remove his arm, then told herself that she didn't want to make an issue of Jud's attention in front of Susie. She maintained that belief even when his fingers lightly stroked her, but she couldn't fight back an unexpected shiver.

"Cold?" Jud murmured.

"Of course not," she replied quickly. It was quite warm today; she certainly couldn't use that for an excuse. "It's the Ferris wheel. Heights always frighten me a little."

"Not me," Susie piped up before giggling excitedly as the car began to descend.

Jud put his arm a little more tightly around Cara's shoulder, and she tried her best not to react. After all, she told herself, the ride wouldn't last forever.

When it ended they all headed in the direction of the roller coaster. This time Jud put Susie and the boys in the same car. He grinned wickedly at Cara as he climbed in beside her, and there was no way she could object without looking foolish.

When the car went click-clacking slowly up the first incline, she held her breath. Rides really did make her nervous. Then suddenly it swooped down the hill with a ferocious burst of energy, gobbling up the track as it went.

Cara cried out in surprise, and she didn't resist when Jud laughed loudly and wrapped his arm around her shoulder again. She glanced at him, embarrassed that she was such a coward, and for a moment their eyes met and held.

"I'm really quite all right," she said, trying to move away from him, but it was literally impossible. The car twisted and turned en route to its destination, and Cara and Jud were frequently thrown shoulder to shoulder.

Jud held her throughout the ride, and though she felt as if she was burning up under his intimate embrace, she endured to the end. But she couldn't get out of the car fast enough, and she pleaded motion sickness through the next several rides.

Waiting on the ground for Jud and the children, she couldn't help but admire him for showing them such a good time. It was obvious that he loved children, and she was impressed by his generosity in giving of himself as well as his money.

On their way to the next ride they came to a shooting gallery. "Are you any good at hitting the targets?" Jud asked, looking at Cara.

She shook her head. "I've never even held a rifle."

"Then I must show you how," he insisted.

Cara wanted to demur, but she was beginning to feel like a spoilsport. "All right," she agreed.

She soon found that she got more than she had bargained for. After they had paid the price to shoot, Jud stepped up behind her and wrapped his arms around her to show her how to hold the gun. She was acutely aware of his touch, his tall, lean body pressing against hers. She could feel his breath on her cheek as he leaned forward, and she could smell the faint scent of his aftershave.

How she ever succeeded in hitting the targets, she never knew, but she managed to knock down enough for a prize. She squealed with delight when the booth attendant offered her any prize on the second shelf.

"What do you want, Susie?" she asked, her brown eyes glowing excitedly behind her glasses.

The child was so thrilled that she was jumping around for joy. "The puppy! The puppy!" she cried. "I want the puppy dog!"

Cara smiled at Jud when she heard his barely perceptible groan. The black and white floppy-eared dog was huge, standing taller than the child, and Jud knew he would have to carry it around the carnival for the rest of the day.

The attendant took it off the shelf and handed it to Jud, and for a few minutes he set it on the ground and let Susie explore and hug it. Cara watched the scene with a warm feeling growing inside her.

Although Susie tried her level best to lift the dog herself, not wanting to let it go for a minute, she finally had to consent to Jud carrying it.

The two hours went by so rapidly that Cara couldn't believe they were almost over when Jud suggested they make a final stop for food. The children had already had cotton candy and ice cream, so this time they all settled on corn dogs dipped in mustard, and colas.

It was with genuine regret that Cara went with Jud to return the children to the orphanage. They hugged and kissed both adults, and Cara looked away, her eyes misty.

For a long time she couldn't speak as she and Jud walked back to the car. When they were at last on their way home, she murmured, "You were wonderful with the children."

He smiled at her. "You weren't too bad yourself for a stuffy old psychologist."

Cara laughed. "You really don't know much about psychologists, do you?"

"Not as much as I want to know," he replied, his tone now serious.

"I wonder if Justin's back at the house by now," Cara said brightly, needing to change the subject. She didn't want Jud to get to know her.

She should have known that the question was sure to silence him, but she hadn't intended it for that purpose. She had only wanted to distract him.

The rest of the trip back passed without another word between them, and when they reached Jud's property, she seized the first topic of conversation that came to mind.

"Oh, look at that colt," she cried. "I saw him yesterday when I arrived. He's such a beauty."

Jud drove inside the fence, then headed in the direction of the young horse. "Would you like to pet him?"

"Could I?" she asked.

"I think so." He parked the car outside the enclosure that housed the animal, and he and Cara got out of the car. The colt picked up his ears as Jud helped Cara climb over the fence, and when they walked toward him, he kicked his heels and ran in the direction of his mother.

No matter how Jud coaxed him forward, he would not come. Soon Cara, walking hand in hand with Jud, was laughing happily, knowing it was futile to pursue the little animal.

"It's hopeless," she insisted. "He's not going to let us touch him."

Jud looked down at her, and their gazes locked for what seemed a brief eternity. She could feel the heat of his breath on her face, and she knew that he was going to kiss her. She told herself frantically that she must resist.

But when his mouth found hers, she couldn't summon the necessary strength to protest. There was something so over-whelming about this man, so intoxicating, so compelling. She could feel the hard length of him molded to her curves and she raised up on tiptoe so that her body might more precisely match his.

He groaned deeply as he lowered his head to more fully claim her mouth. A rush of excitement pulsed through her veins, and Cara foolishly told herself that she would permit herself a single burning kiss.

It had been so long, so very long since a man had touched her like this, stirred her like this. And this man was so thrill-ing.

It was absurd, of course. One kiss only caused her to want more, and when Jud's tongue engaged hers in love play, she met the bold thrusts. His mouth left hers to scorch the tender skin of her neck, and before Cara was even aware of what she was doing, she wrapped her arms around his neck.

His hot kisses teased her unmercifully. They seemed to be everywhere—on her mouth, her eyelids, her neck. There was no way to defend herself against the onslaught, and in truth she did not want to. There was something dangerously erotic and forbidden about this man, and she wanted to explore it to the maximum.

She began to run her fingers over Jud's back, tracing the muscles under his shirt, holding him more tightly to her.

"Cara, Cara, the things you do to me," he whispered thickly.

The sound of his voice, so ragged and full of desire, tugged at what little sanity she still possessed. Just what did she think she was doing here in this man's arms? Had she taken leave of her senses? She didn't want to become involved with him.

What about her loyalty to her project? A major pharmaceutical firm had trusted her and her ability to do a thorough and objective job, and here she was in the arms of one of her subjects. And after she had stressed to Justin so many times that she could not—would not—become involved with the participants of the project.

Justin! He must wonder where on earth she was.

"I can't do this," she mumbled wildly, pulling free of Jud's arms.

"Why not?" he asked huskily, trying to hold her to him.

"Justin—my project," she said in a choked voice. "I've explained that my primary concern is my project. I've got to get back to the house."

Jud pulled her back to him before she could escape, and his dark eyes were blazing when they met hers.

"Then were you only kissing me to further your research?" he asked. "Are you trying to compare my brother's kisses to mine? Or is this your own personal method of studying the bond between twins? I'll bet the firm that commissioned your project doesn't know about this aspect of the research!"

Cara shook her head vehemently, stunned by what he was saying, and before she could respond to his accusations, Jud had again embraced her. This time when his mouth found hers, it was with a passionate intensity that shocked her.

Somehow she found the strength to tear herself away from his grasp, and in minutes she had made her way back over the fence and into the safety of the car, where she waited tensely for Jud to return.

For a long while Jud stared after Cara, trying to rein in his fury. She had him running in circles, and he didn't like it one bit. He wanted her, and she seemed to want him. She had certainly responded to him. Or was it all a game? Was she having an affair with Justin? Was she trying to drive them both crazy? Or was she a woman running from something else?

When he had regained some measure of control, he stalked over to the fence, climbed it, then made his way to the car. Without even looking at Cara he slid behind the wheel, every muscle tense with anger.

"Just what the hell are you trying to do?" he asked in a low voice laced with rage. "Are you playing a game with me? What's between you and my brother? Why do you entice me, then hide behind him and your project?"

He said the words so disdainfully that Cara sucked in her breath. "It hasn't been my intention to entice you," she flung at him defensively. "I came here to conduct research. You're the one who keeps making advances. Why did you invite your brother and me here? What caused the rift between the two of you? If you didn't intend to take some steps toward mending it, why did you invite him?"

She had spoken without thinking, her frustration with herself and him spilling out. She didn't think he would answer, but to her surprise, he did.

"The rift was over a woman both of us apparently seemed to think we wanted," he said. "The problem was that she just happened to be my fiancée."

Then he turned the key in the ignition and started the car,

even more furious with himself for letting her goad him into telling her that ugly little tale.

Cara was taken aback for a moment. She had had no idea what they had quarreled over, but somehow she had never even remotely guessed that it was a woman—and Jud's fiancée at that. She didn't know why she should be so stunned, but she was.

His answer seemed to take the wind out of her sails. "When we get back to the house, Justin and I will leave," she said in a quiet, still voice.

"Leave?" Jud repeated. "Hell, no, you won't leave. You came here to do your damned research, and I mean to see that you finish it. I've done my part—given all the right answers," he said mockingly. "Now what about your part? When do we go over the questionnaires? Where are all the revelations?"

Cara could almost feel her heart sink. She didn't want to think about the questionnaires now, but she would carry on. She wouldn't let him know how shaken she was.

"We'll discuss them as soon as we return to the house," she said tightly. She would get through it somehow; then she would walk out of this bitter man's life forever. That she promised herself. But she knew it would never be that simple. At the moment it seemed that nothing in her life would ever be simple again.

CHAPTER SIX

It seemed like forever before Jud finally parked in front of the house. All Cara could think about was the fact that the two brothers had quarreled over Jud's fiancée. She didn't know why it should assume so much importance to her, but it did. It was, perhaps, the information she needed to help heal the breach between Jud and Justin, but suddenly her goals and objectives seemed blurred.

"I'll meet you in the library in fifteen minutes," Jud stated flatly. Then he got out of the car with brusque movements.

Not waiting for him to open her door, Cara climbed out before he could reach her side.

"Fine," she said as evenly as she could. "I'll get the questionnaires."

Fifteen minutes later she was knocking at the library door. The few minutes' respite had given her some much-needed time to pull herself back together, and after firmly chastising herself for letting her emotions get the best of her, she had come here ready to work.

"Come in," Jud called out.

Determined to put the entire day's events behind her and remain impersonal and professional, Cara adjusted her glasses on her nose and stepped inside.

Jud was stretched out on the couch, a glass of brandy in his hand, a cigar at his lips. Miraculously, his anger had dissipated. He looked very much in control. He also looked intimidatingly masculine, and Cara's heart took on an irregular beat.

"Ready to go over these?" she asked coolly.

Jud indicated the couch. "I'm ready. Sit down."

As Cara did so, he held up his glass. "May I get you something to drink?"

She could use it, she told herself, but she wouldn't allow herself the luxury. She needed to be totally in command of her faculties to deal with this man. She didn't know what to expect next—anger, passion or teasing?

"No, thank you."

She started right in with her facts and observations, vowing that she would be just as cool and composed as he was. If he could pretend nothing had happened between them, then so could she. But for the life of her she couldn't forget that Jud had revealed that a woman had caused him and his brother to become enemies.

"About the similarities between you and Justin," she said crisply. "I have found that familiar twin bond that is so often spoken of. You and he share an amazing number of like qualities and traits."

"And you're going to tell me that it's those old parapsychological phenomena involved in the twin bond, aren't you?" Jud asked wryly.

It did amaze Cara that Jud was discussing the findings as if today's earlier events hadn't happened at all, but she meant to be just as clever and impersonal as he. However, it was difficult, very difficult. She kept remembering how she had felt in his arms, how easily he had stirred her passion.

"I can't offer concrete evidence," she said coolly, not appreciating his disparaging tone, "but yes, I am convinced that it is some form of ESP, which all of us have, incidentally, if we wish to develop it, but not in the degree twins seem to have it."

Jud shook his head as if in doubt, and Cara immediately began to list the similarities between the brothers and happenings that were too rare not to have some extraordinary basis.

"Those incidents do seem unusual," he conceded, "but rare happenings do occur, not just to twins but to the population in general."

Once again Cara was impressed by his knowledge on the twin subject. He had obviously studied it at great length. He was putting forth facts that she had heard researched and presented many times.

Next she was sure he would start with the numbers; she had heard her theory refuted more than one time, and when the party involved hadn't managed to convince her she was all wet, he invariably started throwing averages and statistics at her.

When Jud began to relate the numbers and the natural history of coincidences, she countered smoothly and efficiently by bringing up the fact that specious conclusions were occasionally drawn from numerical data.

"All mathematicians are warned about the bogus power of numbers," she told him breezily. "Don't expect to sway me in my studies. I've interviewed too many people."

"What about the pure and simple fact of genetics?" he asked.

"Of course genetics play a part," she retorted equably. "But there is a tie beyond that. Otherwise it would follow that nontwin brothers and sisters would share the same sense of closeness that twins feel." She shook her head. "No, the twin tie is different, much more special. It can't be explained away genetically."

As Jud watched her on her home ground, with all the facts at her command, he couldn't deny that he admired her dedication to her subject. He doubted if the devil himself could sway her on the matter. He liked that. Too many people backed off when they were put on the spot. He had delved into the twin theory himself, because he was one, and he knew that Cara was up to the minute on her research.

Damnit, he liked this woman, he reminded himself, no matter how crazy she drove him. His anger had run its course, and he had to admit that she had a point about him being the one who kept initiating the flirtation. It wasn't her fault that she had him running in circles. Or was it? He didn't know anymore.

But he knew that he couldn't stop. He still wanted to break through her professionalism and expose the woman beneath. Her response to his kisses had shown him a side of her he was eager to know. If she gave as much attention to herself, to her femininity, as she did to her work, she would be quite a woman. If only he had a guideline, answers on a questionnaire, a map to show him the way to get through to her. If only she weren't married to this damned twin theory. And there was still the problem of Justin—

Always Justin. He became pensive for a short time while Cara waited uncomfortably, wishing she could read his mind.

Then, unexpectedly, he grinned at her. "Let's get on to the actual interview," he said, capitulating all too easily for Cara's peace of mind. She was lining up her second string of defenses, anticipating more arguments against her theory.

Jud leaned closer to her. "Don't you want to know about my dreams, my fantasies? Let me tell you what I dreamed about last night after you ran away from the pond."

"I really don't think that will be necessary," she replied, held captive by his glowing eyes. "I have all the information I need right here." She clutched the questionnaires tighter in her hand.

"Oh, come now, any psychologist worth her salt is interested in her subject's dreams. In this case interpreting them won't be too difficult. Right before I went to bed I was holding this lovely lady in my arms. I was so stirred by my desire for her—which, incidentally, was left unfulfilled—that my unconscious sought satisfaction in my dreams. Let me tell you—"

95

"Don't bother," she said sharply. She didn't want to hear about his dreams. He was talking about her, of course, and just knowing that he had dreamed about her was enough to make her head spin.

"What's wrong?" he asked with a sly smile. "Did I say something I shouldn't have?"

"I have told you repeatedly that I have no intention of becoming personally involved with the subjects in this survey," she said. She was seeking refuge behind a stern mask of pride, but she didn't know if she could keep up the façade. She actually found the thought of his dream incredibly fascinating. She found this man very intriguing—and dangerous.

"Let's get back to the facts, shall we?" she asked stiffly.

Jud grinned again. "You're in charge," he said lazily, but Cara didn't feel that she was in charge at all. She hadn't thought so from the very first time she met him. It was a sad admission to make to herself, and she resented it terribly.

She launched into her usual comments and confirmations of his likeness to his brother, pointing out that as children, both had suffered the same nightmares; both had broken the same arm on the same day; both had dated look-alike blondes in college, before they had ever seen the other's girl and in spite of both of them preferring dark-haired women; both were single; both wanted two children. The list went on and on, but when she had finished, Jud patiently countered with his own list of their differences.

Keeping her mind forcefully on the business at hand, Cara successfully supported her contention that they were much more alike than not. She was in her element and she knew she was the one with the upper hand. Subconsciously she had been trying to find some way to discuss the matter of the woman in the brothers' past.

The opportunities had been slim, but finally she led right into it. "You and Justin even seem to prefer the same women. Can we talk about the woman you quarreled over?"

The minute the question was out, she waited breathlessly. She needed to know the answer; she wanted to know.

He shrugged with deceptive casualness. "That was some time ago. Other women have come and gone since then. I really am not interested in talking about her."

Cara's breath slipped through her lips in a disappointed sigh. Then she tried a new tactic.

"Do you really feel as negatively about marriage as your replies indicate?" she persisted.

"Don't you think *marriage* is a dirty word?" he asked lightly.

Cara was startled by his question. Did *he?* Some of his responses had been so romantic. Why was he negative on the single aspect of marriage? Was that tied to the unhappy incident with his fiancée in his past?

She wanted to press him, but in spite of his light tone, his expression had become serious and brooding. She already knew how he resented someone prying into his life, despite his agreement to participate in her study, and she didn't want to push her luck.

He had been straightforward and honest in all his answers, even if some weren't as complete as she would have liked. That was no different from most people who participated. Even those who seemed most willing to participate managed to keep some part of themselves secret, or simply answered some questions erroneously. She saw now that Jud had used humor in some ways to avoid the painful questions.

Besides, in all honesty, it was her own obsession with the matter and her wish to heal the wound festering between the two brothers that caused her extreme interest in this single facet of his life.

Finally Cara came to the end of her list. "Well, I think that about wraps it up," she said, putting her papers back in order. "I want to thank you for participating, Jud," she said in her most professional, impersonal voice. "I know you were reluctant."

97

She stood up. "I don't believe there's any further reason for me to stay. I'll go and see if I can find Justin."

Jud's eyes roved slowly over her. "I thought you had come for the weekend and weren't leaving until tomorrow morning," he said. "What's the rush? My cook's planned a barbecue on the patio. I've invited people over to meet you. In fact, I'm sure Goldie has the meal well under way by now. You don't want to be responsible for putting the woman to needless work or disappointing the guests, do you? This meal is in your honor. I'd really like you to stay."

Cara vacillated as she met his dark eyes, wishing it were a simple matter of saying no. But it wasn't. Nothing had been simple since she had come to this man's home. She had disliked him. She had liked him. She had not understood him. She had thought she was beginning to. He had run hot and he had run cold, but she wasn't willing to write him off quite yet. She was not willing to let go of the study, of the problem between the brothers—of Jud.

"That's very kind of you," she commented at length, a smile tugging at her lips in spite of her vow to be stern. "I'll stay."

His smile broadened, and Cara quickly stood. The problem with it all was that she wanted very much to stay. And she knew that she should go. Even her reasoning that she could perhaps bring the estranged brothers back together now that she knew what had separated them didn't answer her need to be here.

"I'll see you later then," she murmured.

"Yes, indeed. About four o'clock out on the patio. Wear your shorts. A barbecue has to be informal to be fun."

Cara nodded. Her papers in hand, she walked toward the door. She didn't need to look back to know that Jud was following her with his eyes. She had felt the heat of his gaze too often not to recognize the feeling now. She was more than relieved when she shut the library door behind her.

When Cara went up to Justin's room, she found the door

98

open, but the man was still gone. She didn't know where to look for him. Her steps eventually took her to the pool, and she found him lounging in the sun, watching the cook, Goldie, making preparations for the barbecue.

"Justin," she called out as she crossed the patio, "I've been looking for you."

He slid up in his chair as Cara approached, and she was struck by how handsome he was and how unnerving it was to see two of him everywhere she turned. He was again in his shorts, and his long body was already turning almost the same shade of brown as Jud's.

"Oh, do you still remember me?" he asked with a hint of reproach in his voice. "Since coming here I thought you had forgotten."

"I'm sorry," she murmured. "But you knew when I came that I was here to interview Jud. I'm writing a book, remember?"

"How can I forget?" His dark eyes met hers. "Where were you last night? You didn't answer your door, and I even went out in the yard looking for you." He glanced away to gaze at the shimmering blue water of the pool. "I couldn't find Jud either."

"I'll bet you didn't look too hard for him," she teased lightly, wanting to see him in a good mood and hoping to evade his question.

Justin regarded her warily, then laughed softly. "No, not too hard. I was really looking for you."

"I went to bed early," she said, not exactly lying, but not telling him the whole truth, either.

"And this morning?" he asked.

"Jud and I went to the carnival, but Justin, I looked for you everywhere to see if you wanted to go with us."

"I went riding," he said. "We must have just missed each other."

She reached out and touched his hand. "Jud told me what the two of you quarreled about," she said quietly.

Justin frowned. "What did he say?"

"That the rift came about because of a woman."

Cara watched as Justin stiffened. She felt that she could almost touch his tension. "Is that all he said?"

"He said the woman had been his fiancée," Cara said softly, inexplicably feeling her throat close at the words.

Was it her imagination, or did Justin blanch? She touched his hand again to make him look at her. "Will you talk to me about it now?"

He shrugged. "Jud told you. There's not much more to say."

Cara fought with herself to keep from getting exasperated with him. "Why did it happen, Justin? Did you both meet her at the same time? Was she attracted to you? There has to be more to the story."

A deep frown furrowed his smooth brow. "What does it matter?" he asked sharply. "It was three years ago."

"It matters," she said in a tight voice, "because it has made the two of you enemies."

A scowl scarred his handsome features. "I've told you I can't talk about it."

Cara drew in her breath. She didn't want to fight with Justin. He had been so good to her, so generous with his time. The last thing on her mind was alienating him; she told herself that she wanted to help, not make things worse.

"Did you know we're having guests at the barbecue Goldie is preparing for dinner?" she asked, changing the subject.

He shook his head. "No, but then no one tells me anything here. I might as well not exist."

Cara sat down on the edge of a lounge chair near his and patted his hand. "I'm glad you're here. Thank you for coming with me. I can't begin to tell you how much help you've been to me with the book. I won't forget it. You'll see when the book comes out."

To Cara's relief, his dark eyes brightened. "Are you going to be grateful enough to dedicate the book to me?"

Cara's sweet laughter washed over them. "I am, in fact, but it was to be a surprise."

Unexpectedly Justin grabbed her hand and held it. "Cara, don't be too influenced by anything Jud tells you. You can see how he despises me, and he must know that I care for you."

"Justin, please," she said, drawing her hand back and glancing at the cook, who was bustling around picnic tables set up by the pool. "We've been through this. I think you're very special and I value your friendship, but I'm not looking for anything beyond friendship."

He sighed in exasperation. "Give me a chance, Cara. That's all I'm asking for—a chance." He leaned closer to her. "You know you're attracted to me. You're the psychologist here. Let your guard down a little."

"Justin, you are a very attractive man. I'm the first to admit it," she said frankly. "But I'm not interested in a fling and I just don't feel that way about you."

"How do you know you don't feel *that* way about me and how do you know it would be a fling? What we have here might be something of real value. Don't be so damned negative without giving it a chance."

"My first concern is my book. You know that." She was beginning to sound like a broken record. First one brother, then the other, and now the first again. With a surge of guilt she realized that if she were interested in a fling, Jud would be the brother of her choice. But she would be horrified if Justin guessed her thoughts.

"Yes," he interrupted, "but you'll be through with the book one of these days. Don't you have a life beyond that book?"

His question surprised her. "Yes, of course," she replied. "I plan to go into private practice. That's why I got an education. I want to help people. I want to do something

101

with underprivileged children. I'm not sure where yet, but I definitely will work."

Justin shook his head as if she were hopeless. "I wasn't talking about work. Is that all you think about? Don't you have a personal life? Don't you want one?"

Cara smiled in spite of herself. She *had* assumed he was talking about work. "You make work sound so pathetic. The poor little career girl with no other choices. *Your* career is the basis of *your* life."

"Yes," he quickly agreed. "The *basis*—not my entire life. Your attitude doesn't sound very healthy to me."

Cara laughed gently, her brown-gold eyes glowing. For the last year all her life had consisted of was the book, and before that she had been involved in her schooling and her plans for the book. She had chosen to have no other life.

"Perhaps I'm the one who needs a psychologist," she said playfully, feeling disturbed by his probing and wanting to avoid it. "Are you offering your services?"

"Finally, you're asking," he said, beginning to applaud.

Cara broke into laughter.

He was laughing with her when Jud walked out onto the patio. His gaze darted in their direction before he smiled stiffly. Then he went to speak to the cook.

Cara's gaze followed him. He was breathtakingly sexy dressed in a black boxer-style bathing suit. His body was more defined than Justin's and hairier. As she stared at him, she felt that flush of warmth again.

She could sense Justin watching her, and she quickly turned her attention back to him. "I'd better go change," she said. "It must be almost time for the guests, and I understand this is to be a shorts-and-swimsuit affair."

Justin laughed a little. "I told you Jud wouldn't know fancy if it hit him in the face. These kinds of affairs are what he always has. It was at one of these gatherings that . . ."

His words trailed off, much to Cara's regret. What had he

102

meant to say? Was it at one of these dos that he and Jud had quarreled over the woman in their past?

When she looked at him, she knew she would never hear what he had started to say. "I'd better scoot," she said brightly. "I don't want to be the only one dressed here."

Justin nodded, but Cara could see he was lost in introspection and she felt very sorry for him. It was wrong of Jud to refuse to speak to him because of a single misunderstanding that had occurred years ago. Justin was truly sorry for the breach between them. It was written all over him.

She glanced back in Jud's direction. Surely he wasn't so implacable that his brother's genuine regret for his actions wouldn't melt his cold heart. As she watched him help Goldie spread the food out on the tables, she promised herself that she would try one more time to mend the tear in the twins' relationship. Justin wanted it, and she knew it would benefit Jud.

Her mind made up, she returned to her room, freshened her makeup and put on a jade green shorts outfit. The pants were stylishly done and the matching top was quite long, so that it almost covered the shorts. She toyed with the idea of leaving her hair in braids but at the last moment undid them. When she had brushed it, her hair tumbled down around her shoulders in appealing waves. The effect was pleasant, and she smiled as she adjusted her glasses on her small nose and went back to the patio.

Jud was still at the picnic tables helping Goldie, but when he saw Cara, he crossed the patio to greet her. "You look lovely," he murmured, his gaze skimming down her outfit.

"Thank you," she replied with much more calm than she was feeling. The guests were arriving, and Cara was pleased to see Libby among them. Jud waved when he saw the woman and her family, and he guided Cara in their direction to introduce her to Raymond.

"You didn't need to have us over," the burly man said

shyly. It was obvious that he was uncomfortable socializing with the boss, despite Jud's desire to make him feel at home.

"You know you're always welcome, Raymond," Jud said warmly. "I thought the boys might enjoy it."

"Can we swim in the pool?" little Judson asked.

Jud nodded. "Of course you can." The four adults jumped back when both boys plunged over the side, splashing water everywhere.

"Boys!" Raymond said sternly, his face reddening as his sons surfaced. "You should have gone down the steps."

Jud broke into hearty laughter. "Let them have fun, Raymond," he said. "That's what they're here for. You and Libby go over and get a drink. Find a seat and make yourselves at home. You know all the others who'll be coming."

Jud turned when another couple walked out onto the patio. "Excuse us," he said, then he ushered Cara toward them. "This is Dr. Charles Hudson, one of our local psychiatrists, and his wife, Mellie."

Cara didn't miss the proprietary arm Jud put around her shoulders, but she ignored it to extend her hand, first to the attractive woman, then to the carefully groomed man. They were both in shorts, but Cara could tell it wasn't their normal attire. The doctor's shorts were a sedate plaid and obviously new. "It's so nice to meet you," she said sincerely.

"We've heard about you and your book," the doctor said with a grin. "So you're trying to defy the profession's opinion on twins."

Cara laughed. "I'm just trying to substantiate what my studies have shown me."

They chatted for a few minutes, then Jud took her over to other arriving guests, this time three young women in their early twenties, all dressed in yellow shorts, yellow and white striped tops and huge yellow hats. "Cara Stevens," he said, "these ladies—"

She held up her hand. "We've met," she exclaimed de-

104

lightedly, smiling at the women. "The Watson twins, Linda and Laurie, and younger sister, LuAnn."

The three blond women began to laugh. "We didn't tell Jud," they explained all at once. "We wanted to let him think he'd really made a find for you. He explained all about your book and your research when he invited us."

Jud chuckled. "You naughty girls," he growled teasingly. "I should throw you all into the pool."

"We just had our hair done," one twin exclaimed. "And promptly covered our heads with hats," the other added. Spying Justin, the women wandered away amid their own laughter.

"One of my cases in point," Cara said. "Those twins have a very special bond."

"And it even extends to cover their sister, who's a year younger," Jud said with a touch of irony in his voice. "There must have been some ESP left over in the womb."

"Oh, Jud." Cara groaned. "You're an impossible skeptic. I've already shown you that you and Justin share something special that the rest of us don't have."

Jud glanced in his brother's direction. Justin was busily amusing the Watson sisters. "Yes, we've shared something special," he said sarcastically.

"Jud," she said cautiously, "isn't it time you abandoned these bad feelings? Justin's your brother. He—"

"Did someone request your services as a psychologist?" he asked quietly, his dark eyes hard.

She shook her head. "No, but—"

"Then do us both a favor and don't offer them in this matter."

Biting her tongue to keep herself quiet, Cara met his stern eyes. "One day you'll be sorry you've shut him out," she was unable to resist adding.

Jud's firm fingers closed on her elbow. "Come and meet the guests," he said, ignoring her remark. "Step right this way."

They walked over to an elderly man conspicuously out of place in the midst of the other casually dressed guests. Slim and dapper, he was dressed in a summer suit, replete with tie. Cara was immediately reminded of Justin as she looked at the perfectly attired old gentleman.

"Grampa Garrett," Jud said in a very loud voice, "this is Cara Stevens, the lady who's writing the book."

The old man cupped his right ear with his hand. "Beg your pardon?" he said loudly.

Jud ushered Cara closer. "Cara Stevens, the lady who's writing the book on twins."

Grampa Garrett nodded and tapped his cane idly on the patio stones. "My grandsons are twins, you know—Justin and Judson. That's my name," he said, pointing proudly to himself, "Judson. This fella's named after me." He patted Jud gently on his back. "Judson Garrett."

Cara smiled warmly, but she couldn't help wondering if Justin, too, was named after a relative. Was Grampa's obvious preference for his namesake part of Justin's problem?

As though to show her that he wasn't partial to Jud, Grampa continued. "Judson took my name and Justin took my profession. I'm a retired lawyer."

Cara nodded. "I see," she said, and she couldn't help but think that Justin had deliberately tried to emulate the old man, from career to clothes. Did he admire his grandfather that much, or had it been a deliberate bid for attention?

"Excuse me," Jud said loudly. "I've got to bring some music out here."

"I think I'm going to like you," Grampa Garrett said without preliminaries.

Cara smiled. At least this Garrett had a positive attitude. She promptly sat down with the old man and began to talk animatedly about her favorite subject—twins.

Mr. Garrett proved to be an apt conversationalist when he heard Cara's comments correctly, and she was happy to learn that Justin had been named after his father. The minutes wore on and Cara found herself wanting to speak intimately about the old man's grandsons. She was sure he could shed some light on their characters and maybe even on the rift that had separated the brothers. But she didn't know how to approach the subject since she had to speak so loudly in order to be heard.

Finally someone put some pop music on the stereo that had been wheeled outside, and Cara was able to ask the question she wanted. "What do you think about the split between your grandsons?" she murmured.

"Hey?" he asked, his hand cupped to his ear.

"How do you feel about your grandsons' hostility toward each other?"

He waved a hand. "Ridiculous! Inexcusable!"

"I guess Jud must have loved the woman very much," Cara said, hoping she wouldn't have to repeat that remark.

"Baa!" he said, waving his hand again. "He loved his brother more."

Cara was taken aback for a moment. It wasn't that the fact hadn't occurred to her; it had. But not so simply, so plainly, without adornment or speculation. Was that the case, then? She was certain that Jud had loved the woman, but *had* he loved his brother more? Wasn't it more evidence of the twin bond? Her mind flashed back over the questionnaires he had answered. They had shown the same extraordinary tie from birth that most of her other twins had exhibited. Jud must have been shattered to know that his trusted twin, his other half, had wanted the woman he had planned to marry, the woman he loved. The fact must have hurt him in the most intimate and damaging way possible.

She glanced across the patio and saw Justin frolicking with the Watson sisters, his smile broad, his eyes shining. His glance caught hers, and she was aware that he wanted her to see him with the women. She returned his smile, then gave her attention back to Grampa, but she couldn't draw him out any more about his grandsons. He obviously loved them both, and it hurt him too much to talk about the breach.

Cara had to ask one last question. "What was Jud's fiancée like?"

"Brenda? Beautiful," Grampa said simply.

Although Cara had suspected it, Grampa's confirmation bothered her. Tactfully she changed the subject.

Before long Jud strolled back over to them. "Let's eat," he announced loudly, and soon everyone was lined up at the tables.

"This looks wonderful," Cara told him as he stood behind her. The wooden tables were laden with hot barbecued beef, cole slaw, steaming sesame seed buns, fried potatoes and an assortment of beverages from tea to hard liquor.

"Goldie's a good cook," he remarked, his stern tone of a few minutes earlier gone. "She likes to please my guests."

He moved a little closer to her, and she could feel the heat from his nearly nude body. "I like to please them, too, when they'll let me."

His words sent a flush of excitement up Cara's body, but she returned flippantly, "I'm sure most of them don't object. You must keep quite busy pleasing them all."

She looked up at him, and the teasing light in his eyes and the smile on his lips stirred her senses. He was so intensely masculine that she was much too aware of him. She was glad when one of the Watson twins came up behind them.

"This looks real good, Jud. Thanks for inviting us."

"It's my pleasure," he assured her, and Cara was faintly disappointed when she saw him give the woman the same warm smile he had given her seconds ago. It seemed to be a personality trait of handsome men, she reminded herself. She glanced around the patio and saw that Justin was still laughing with LuAnn, the twins' younger sister. His eyes met Cara's again, and she sighed tiredly. He was wasting his time if he meant to put on a show to make her jealous.

"Cara?"

108

She spun back around to face Jud. "Yes?"

"I asked what you wanted to drink." She could see from his expression that he was displeased with her again, and she briefly closed her eyes. Had he seen her looking at Justin and misconstrued her interest? Being here with these two men who were at each other's throats was beginning to get on her nerves. She would be glad when the morning came and she could get back to concentrating totally on her book.

But would that be possible? she asked herself. Could she write about Jud and not have him come to mind? Not feel the warmth of his breath on her cheek or the touch of his fingers on her skin?

He snapped his fingers, and she blinked. "Cara, are you there?" he asked, looking at her questioningly. "What do you want to drink?"

"Oh, I am sorry," she murmured. "I was daydreaming."

"Apparently," he said.

She reached down for a glass of iced tea and put it on the tray she had been given, then continued down the line, filling her plate with tempting items from the selection offered.

When she and Jud had served themselves, they found a place at the picnic table with the doctor and his wife. Goldie was preparing Grampa's plate and he soon joined them, using his cane to help settle in on the bench.

"This looks marvelous," he boomed to Jud, his deafness making him unaware of how loud he was. "We should do it more often. We used to have family get-togethers like this all the time," he commented, looking from Cara to the others. "Of course," he continued, "the boys' mama and papa were alive then."

He shook his head. "They would be real sorry to see what a mess these children have gotten themselves into. Not speaking for years! Why, it's disgraceful, and them being blood kin."

"Grampa," Jud said, "how's your sandwich?"

"Well, I don't know, son. I haven't tasted it yet."

109

"Try it," Jud said, smiling a little at having distracted the old man, who promptly picked up his sandwich and began to eat.

"It is delicious," Cara said, after tasting her own sandwich. She was delighted to be here among other people for a change. Having to sit through those trying meals with Jud and Justin was wearing her down.

"How long will you be here?" Mellie asked, her blue eyes glowing with interest.

"I'll return to California in three weeks. I'm about to wrap up the project," Cara said, holding up her crossed fingers. "If all goes well, I'll be finished with the manuscript in two weeks."

Jud chuckled. "Crossing the fingers for good luck seems a little inappropriate for a psychologist, doesn't it?" He looked at Dr. Hudson. "What do you make of it, Doc? Pure superstition, wouldn't you say?"

Charles Hudson grinned. "I always say whatever works, Jud. I can't condemn the practice."

"Quacks," Jud teased. "You're supposed to rely only on your scientific expertise."

Everyone laughed, and Justin picked just that moment to come to the table, LuAnn at his side. He glanced at the others, then settled down across from Cara.

She was becoming more and more aware of his insecurity, and it bothered her. She realized it must seem to him that she was deliberately spending every moment with Jud, and the last thing she wanted to do was upset him. Justin had been a good friend to her; she felt a great loyalty toward him, and she wanted to see him happy again.

"Isn't this a good party?" she asked, smiling at him.

He flashed her a winning smile. "Super," he said, but his deep voice was tinged with sarcasm.

The Watson twins were the last to seat themselves, choosing the table with Raymond and his family and Goldie. Cara glanced at them and smiled. When her gaze strayed to their

110

plates to see if they had selected the same thing, Linda playfully shook her finger at the psychologist.

"We see you looking at our food," they said in unison, and everyone laughed again.

"No fair making notes at the table," Jud teased.

Cara smiled. "It's the writing disease. A writer has to be alert to everything that may be of value to her work, every moment. Those two women are of value to me."

"And aren't we two men?" Justin asked, his dark eyes dancing mischievously.

"My favorite subjects," Cara admitted with rare candor, but she was glad when the conversation turned to Jud's horses.

"I'm going to Texas to buy a stallion I've been interested in for some time," he commented, and Cara felt an unsettling sensation in the pit of her stomach. Would she ever see this man again? She knew the question shouldn't disturb her in the least, but it did. Deeply.

"How long will you be gone, Jud?" Mellie asked.

"About a week. Most of the deal has already been worked out, but I want to pick up the horse myself. He's a real prize," he said, his voice animated.

"I'm eager to see him," the woman replied. "You'll have to invite us out when you bring him home."

"Oh, most definitely you'll have to come out and see him," Jud said. He glanced at Cara, and she harbored the foolish hope that he would invite her, but he didn't.

"And how's your work, Justin?" Mellie said, directing her conversation to the other twin. "I hear you're doing real well and that people are asking for you when they do business with Tate, Gibson, and Tate. Why the first thing you know, it'll be Tate, Gibson, Tate, and Garrett."

"Yes," LuAnn said. "Especially if he marries Mr. Gibson's daughter. How's that romance looking, Justin?"

He winked at her. "You know the ladies can't resist me."

"When will Susan be back from Europe?" she asked, and

Cara glanced interestedly at him, wondering if he was involved with the woman. She noted that Justin carefully avoided her eyes.

He shrugged. "In a week or two, I believe."

LuAnn nodded, and the conversation shifted to the discoveries Cara had made in her research. For the better part of an hour she kept the others fascinated and entertained with her twin tales and the truly amazing facts she had uncovered.

They were especially impressed with the story of the brothers who had been reared apart and lived a thousand miles away from each other but discovered upon being interviewed by her that they drove the same make and model car, that both worked as mechanics, that each had married a blonde named Jane on the same day and that each had two sons whose names were remarkably similar.

When they had finished eating the guests sat around the pool at shaded tables and drank whiskey sours. Cara thoroughly enjoyed herself, and she was all too sorry when the party began to break up. Soon everyone had gone, and she was left with the two remote brothers.

But she was feeling too relaxed and content to let their hostility ruin the evening for her. And just perhaps, she told herself hopefully, if she left them alone, they would start to work out their differences.

"If you two will excuse me," she murmured politely, "I think I'll go to my room. It was a lovely party, but it's been a long day for me."

Both nodded and made the appropriate comments as she stood. As she made her way across the patio, she was uncomfortably aware that the two men were both staring after her. At last she opened the door to the breakfast room, and only when she had slipped inside did she let herself look back at the brothers. They were still sitting at the umbrella-shaded table, but one was looking off in one direction and one in the other.

Cara pursed her lips unhappily and made her way down the hall to her room. She suspected that she was fighting a losing battle, but she just couldn't seem to make herself give up.

CHAPTER SEVEN

Although it was much too early to go to sleep for the night, Cara tried her best to take a short rest. However, it was a useless exercise. Her thoughts filled with both Jud and Justin, she twisted and turned against the satin spread. She thought of a hundred ways she could lure the brothers back together, but not a single one sounded plausible when she imagined carrying it to conclusion.

The problem shook her faith in her own ability in her chosen profession, and that bothered her deeply. The situation seemed clear cut enough: two brothers had broken with each other over an incident that had hurt one of them very much.

Time had passed. If the wounding brother was truly repentant and wanted to heal the split, and if the injured brother really loved the one who had erred, couldn't they begin to care for each other again? That happened all the time.

But what could trigger a reconciliation, and why couldn't she find the spur? Was the twin tie so close that it made mending the tear impossible once the tie had been cut?

Her thoughts chased each other around until she didn't want to deal with them anymore. She got up and went into the living room to inspect the selection of books housed there. Perhaps she would find something she wanted to read. As she searched through the shelves, she was amazed to find books by Freud, Jung, Skinner and a host of other psychologists. It was no wonder Jud seemed to know so much about her subject.

But she wanted to be distracted; she didn't want to read more of what occupied most of her time. What she would have liked was a good romance or even a mystery, but she saw none of those.

Sighing in disappointment, she glanced around the room, hoping to see a magazine that might be appealing. Her gaze strayed to the piano and lingered. She had studied piano, but she hadn't played in some time. She wondered if Jud would mind her using it. She knew some people were very particular about things like that.

She stared at the beautiful piano for a moment, then went in search of Jud. He wasn't out on the patio where she had left him, and when she rapped at the study door, there was no answer. She went into the kitchen to see if Goldie knew where he was, and the woman suggested she look in his room.

It was the one place Cara hadn't thought to look. She hadn't heard him return, but perhaps she had dozed off for a minute or two without realizing it when she was trying to rest. A faint hope stirred in her that he might be in Justin's room, finally talking with his brother, but when she knocked on the door next to her own, a deep, gravelly voice answered.

"Who is it?"

"Cara."

"Come on in."

She hesitated, then opened the door and entered. The blinds had been drawn, and it was almost totally dark in the room. Several seconds passed before Cara's eyes adjusted well enough for her to see the form of the tall man stretched out on the bed.

He was lying there dressed only in blue jeans, his hands behind his head, waiting for her to speak. Cara could feel her pulse race in her veins at the mere sight of him. Half-clothed like that, against the black spread, he reminded her of a dangerous, sexy demon on his home ground in the sinfully appealing black and silver surroundings.

She glanced around the room, noting the ornate black Chinese night tables that matched the mammoth bed Jud was on. Her gaze skimmed down the silver-colored Persian rug with its dramatic black figures, then glanced off the gorgeous silver draperies topped by a black border. Lordy, lordy, she told herself, making love in this room would cause the imagination to do all kinds of things.

Her eyes raked over the length of Jud's long body, then became riveted on his naked chest covered with hair as black as the furniture. She licked her lips, nervous now that she was in the privacy of his room.

Forget the room, she thought to herself, the man alone would be enough to make loving an adventure never to be forgotten. Making love with him would cause the body to do all kinds of thrilling things. She shook her head slightly, trying to free herself of her thoughts.

"I hope I can do something for you," Jud said, and Cara sensed that he was enjoying her confused reaction. He was *already* doing something to her.

"I wondered if I might play your piano," she murmured, at last remembering why she had come. It hadn't been just to stand here and stare at this man. Her voice sounded soft and breathy in the large room. But then that was probably because she couldn't breathe here.

Jud smiled lazily at her. "Is that all you want?"

"Yes," she answered quickly. Why had he imagined she had come?

"Well, I just don't think I can deny you anything." He raised up and swung his legs over the side of the bed. Cara fought the urge to step back out into the hall.

"You can play with anything I have," Jud said. "Anything. You just let me know when you're ready."

There it was again, that unmistakable sexual innuendo,

116

and Cara refused to acknowledge it. "Thank you." Then she turned on her heel and started out into the hall, but Jud's husky voice caused her to look back over her shoulder.

"Is this yours?"

He was holding out a small diamond earring. Cara automatically felt both ears for her diamond studs. One was missing.

"Yes, it is."

"I found it in the car," he murmured.

Cara could feel the color creep up to her cheeks. It must have come loose when he kissed her in the meadow. For a moment she just stood and stared at him. "Well, come and get it," he said tauntingly.

It was the very last thing she wanted to do, but on the other hand, she did want the earring. Her parents had given the diamonds to her when she graduated from college. She forced herself to cross the room to his bed.

Jud was sitting there grinning like a Cheshire cat, and when Cara tried to take the diamond from his hand, he grabbed her with the other one and drew her in between his parted legs.

"I had it under my pillow," he murmured. "You know, sort of like leaving a tooth for the tooth fairy and waiting for something in return. I fell asleep and dreamed about you." His dark eyes pinned hers. "Don't you want to interpret the dream for me this time?"

Cara forced a faint smile to her lips. "I doubt very seriously if your dreams need interpretation. I'm sure they're all quite straightforward and uncomplicated."

He laughed softly. "Well, in truth, this one certainly was. It began where we left off at the—"

"I don't wish to hear about it, thank you," she said breathlessly. She hadn't felt so excited by a man's mere presence since Lance. Lance had made her care for him. Then he had left her. She was a fast learner; she didn't need a repeat of the lesson. She only wanted to get out of here.

117

Jud's muscled thighs held her captive, and he had dropped the earring on the bed so that he could put both hands around her waist. With a strength Cara hadn't known she possessed, she pried his fingers away and twisted out of his possession. He was still staring at her as she picked up the earring and fled. She had a wild vision of him racing after her, flinging her down on the bed and madly making love to her.

But she wasn't fast enough to escape his parting comment. "If you need anything else, just let me know. I want to be of all the help I can."

Telling herself that she had had all the help from him she could stand, Cara continued down the hall, pretending not to hear him.

When she had seated herself at the piano, a curious peace settled over her immediately. She had once considered making music her life, but her curiosity about human nature had steered her in another direction. Her fingers stroked the keys with a natural grace, and soon she was skillfully playing pieces she loved.

It was just a matter of time until Jud strolled into the living room. At least he had a shirt on this time, Cara noted, but the contentment she had experienced evaporated instantly; she was glad she had known a short period of time alone at the piano.

He leaned his elbows on top of the instrument, propped up his chin and looked down at her. Her fingers had frozen over the keys.

"Don't stop. You play very well. I'm impressed. Oddly enough, it's one of the talents I always said I'd hope to find in a wife." His eyes glowed wickedly. "But then you know that, don't you? You read it on my answer sheet."

Yes, she had read that, but she hadn't remembered it. Surely he didn't think that was the reason she was out here playing. How ridiculous, she chastised herself. She *hadn't* remembered. The man was driving her insane and loving every minute of it.

"That's fine," she said coolly. "I admire a man who appreciates the arts, but I really think you'd be better off to think in terms of love."

"Oh?" His dark brows rose a fraction of an inch. "Is that your criterion for marriage? Love?"

"It would help, I believe."

"Have you researched it?"

Damn him! "There are some things that don't have to be researched, Jud," she said evenly. "Love is one of them."

"Too bad," he murmured, his gaze penetrating. "I wanted to take part in the study."

He was teasing her—or would it be more appropriate to say he was tormenting her? Cara made herself turn her attention to the keys again, and she played a fast number she hoped would drown out his deep voice and tempt him to leave.

To her chagrin, he sat down beside her on the piano bench, his long leg touching her thigh, his arm so close that it brushed hers, and began to play right along with her. Without a word passing between them, they moved into a bawdy boogie-woogie tune that should have rocked the rafters.

The more furiously Cara played, the more determinedly Jud tried to top her. Their fingers flew across the keys, creating music that reverberated through Cara's body. It was a crazy contest with no winner.

When it was over they looked at each other and broke into riotous laughter. Before the laughter died on Cara's lips, Jud lowered his head and lifted a kiss from her mouth. "Are you the marrying kind, Cara?" he asked unexpectedly when he had drawn away.

The question effectively eradicated the rapport they had established. Cara stood as if he had struck her. He was teasing her again, and she couldn't handle that kind of teasing.

Not from him. He was right when he said she couldn't handle heat. He was fire, sure to scorch and burn her. Not that she had any intention of getting involved with him, she told herself firmly. She wasn't interested in a casual affair, and she was sure he took these things way too lightly. Hadn't he asked her if *marriage* was a dirty word?

"I think I should go back to my room," she murmured, and before he could tell her she was running away, she headed toward the door. Because she wasn't paying attention, she crashed right into Justin.

For a single stunned moment she glanced up into his brooding eyes. Seeing his troubled expression, she wanted to say something soothing, but she was too upset herself to know what. She shook her head, then rushed madly down the hall to the safety of her room. She was sorry she had agreed to stay the night, but she wouldn't try to back out now. It was a matter of hours and then she would never see Jud again.

Never. It sounded like such a long time. Such a long and lonely time. Cara sat on the edge of her bed, but she knew she couldn't stay in her room. She was too restless. What she needed was a long walk.

She left her room, quietly shutting the door behind her, then went out the front door and stepped into the yard. Dusk was settling on the land, but there would be half an hour of daylight yet.

Cara gazed at the pond longingly. The walk there would do her good. Perhaps it would aid her in sleeping. Her goal in mind, she set out in the direction of the water.

When she reached it, she sat down on the grass beneath the willow tree where Jud had tried to kiss her, and instead of finding solace at this beautiful spot, she became more unhappy.

She had only known Jud for two days, but she felt a terrible loss knowing she would never see him again after tomorrow. Logic didn't enter into it. She couldn't explain it. She

120

just knew that she was leaving some part of her here at this ranch, some part of her that would always belong here.

Reminding herself that she was just overtired, she lay back against the tree trunk and gave herself up to the night sounds all around her. The babbling brook talked to her softly, gently, luring her away on its shimmering wings, and Cara closed her eyes. Soon she had drifted into a semi-slumberous state.

The kiss that touched her mouth was as soft as a butterfly's caress. Still half asleep, Cara brushed at it distractedly. She was too content to be disturbed. The next kiss was longer, and abruptly she opened her eyes wide.

"Jud!" she cried against his mouth.

He leaned back on his hands and looked at her. "In the flesh." Then he smiled. "I knew you would be here waiting for me."

"No," she protested. "You're mistaken. I didn't come here to wait for you."

She started to get up, but Jud pulled her against him. "Why do you run every time I touch you?" he demanded. "Is it Justin? Stop playing games with me. I want to know what's between you and him. Are you having an affair with him? Or have you had one and feel too guilty to make love to both of us?"

"No," she cried. "I haven't played games with you. I told you right from the first why I was here, and that I would not become personally involved with my subjects."

"Don't give me that," he taunted. "I know he's interested in you. I see it every time he looks at you. He wouldn't be taking part in your book if he didn't have other hopes. He can't see any attractive woman without trying to get her to go to bed with him. What I want to know is did he succeed with you?"

He had tried, of course, Cara had to admit. She suddenly recalled Justin asking her not to believe everything Jud said about him because Jud hated him.

"I have never gone to bed with Justin, but he's not the man you want to believe he is," she said defensively.

"Why do you think he's not married at twenty-nine?" Jud demanded. "He can't make a commitment. He wants attention so desperately that he keeps adding to his list of conquests in bed, thinking all these women love him."

"And what about you?" she flung at him. "You're not married." Her heart was beating wildly. What would he say in his own defense?

"Neither are you," he answered, smoothly turning the tables on her. "What are you afraid of?"

Immediately Cara thought of Lance Madison and their aborted love affair, but Jud continued ruthlessly. "Are you one of those psychologists who safely analyzes others' lives from a distance but never dares to examine her own?"

Cara was taken aback, but Jud didn't even give her time to catch her breath. "People aren't just cerebral beings. They have a soul and a heart. Before you try to straighten out what's wrong in my brother's life and my life, examine your own for a minute. What's a twenty-five-year-old woman like you doing living half a life—conducting psychological studies, snooping and prying into other people's lives, living vicariously?"

Although she didn't look into his eyes, Cara could feel his dark gaze burning into her as he talked. "Stop hiding behind your glasses and shallow men like Justin who can't possibly hold your interest long term. Live life. Go out and fall in love," he said with conviction. "Not only is it fun but it's a great means of self-discovery."

Before she had time to digest what he had said, he reached out and took off her glasses. She was still staring at him, lips parted in surprise, when his mouth claimed hers.

As though he meant to give her a demonstration of how to both live life and fall in love, he drew her down beside him onto the carpet of green grass. Her mind still confused by his revelations, Cara could hardly think, much less offer any

122

protest. And if she told herself the truth, she didn't want to. She had rejected her sexuality for so very long, and he was forcing her to recognize it once again.

She was acutely aware of every hard line of Jud's muscled body as he entwined his legs with hers, drew her against him and teased her with his mouth. His lips were forceful and urgent as he scattered kisses over her face, and when Cara caught one with her mouth, Jud dipped into the sweet opening with his tongue.

This was what Cara had wanted, hungered for, longed for, since Jud had so boldly provoked her sleeping passion with his longing looks and his stirring caresses. She sighed softly in surrender as he eased her onto her back and leaned over her. His long fingers unbuttoned the buttons on her blouse, and in less than a heartbeat he had found her upturned nipples and tasted the throbbing peaks. Cara closed her eyes and gave herself up to the exquisite sensations building inside her.

When she felt the zipper of her shorts give under Jud's insistent fingers, she opened her eyes. A full moon was high in the sky, and for an inane moment she tried to recall some ditty about June moons and falling in love. Jud was right: she should live her life, but would her heart dare to believe in love again—to fall in love? To risk the hurt and the pain?

Jud eased her pants down her legs, his warm mouth following the path, trailing tantalizing kisses along the smooth, curvy length, and the sensations Cara was experiencing soon obliterated the nagging fear stirring in her mind. Reason was rapidly left behind on the road to passion as clever fingers slid the single last lacy shred of protection down her legs.

Breathless, trembling, Cara sensed she was on the verge of her greatest adventure—a voyage of self-discovery that she had never imagined—and Jud was going to be her guide.

His mouth made a return path up her silken thighs, and she gasped in surprise at the erotic pleasures that awaited her when he explored the heart of her femininity.

"Jud," she said softly, clasping his broad shoulders with her hands.

He continued his skilled seduction, barely giving her time to catch her breath before some new and bold caress sent shivers up her spine. The flame he had ignited inside her became a fire burning higher and higher, until Cara feared she would be totally consumed by the blaze. She tried to draw her lover up to her, but Jud continued to savor the delights of her shapely body, tasting and stroking, causing her senses to run riot and her passion to burgeon out of bounds. She was a woman too long denied the sensual pleasures, and he was a man schooled in the ways of love.

He took delight in introducing Cara to joys she hadn't fully experienced, seeking out sensitive areas of her body, kissing her inner thighs until they quivered, teasing the tender skin of her stomach with his tongue traveling lazily up her body, pausing to sample her navel with his lips and teeth, then trailing a finger around her breasts.

His mouth returned to hers briefly, then he eased over on his back beside her. "Undress me," he commanded in a soft, husky voice.

Cara found herself more than eager to comply. Her trembling fingers barely able to ease the buttons from the buttonholes, she somehow managed to get Jud's shirt off his magnificent body. He was watching her, his eyes dark with passion, and though Cara wanted to take her time, to tease and arouse him as he had done her, she was too excited.

She managed to undo his belt and unzip his jeans, then she leaned back on her heels in dismay, wondering how she was expected to get his pants down those impossibly long legs.

Jud laughed softly, and Cara looked at him, seeing his expression clearly in the golden glow from the moon. "You're beautiful," he murmured. "Beautiful. Do you know that?"

She couldn't honestly remember anyone ever telling her

that, but she believed it when Jud said it. She wanted to be beautiful for him. He reached out and drew her down to kiss her lips, then freed her so that he could slip his jeans off.

To her surprise, Cara saw that he wasn't wearing shorts. Her first instinct was to look away, but Jud clasped her hands in his and drew them to parts of his body he wanted her to touch.

Slowly, expertly, he guided her to areas that gave him pleasure. "That's good," he whispered hoarsely. "So good."

His excitement caused Cara's own passion to heighten. She wanted to please him, to give him joy.

She was momentarily surprised when he kissed her mouth again, then drew her head down to his body, but she began to kiss him, to stroke him, to taste him as he had done her, moving lower and lower physically, rising higher and higher on wings of desire.

Abruptly he pulled her down on his body and she sucked in her breath as she encountered his masculine form. He held her by the nape as his mouth moved against hers, urgent and hungry, drinking of her sweetness as if she were vital to his life.

She could feel every muscle and contour of him, hard and demanding beneath her pliable curves, and involuntarily, in a rhythm as old as time, her hips began to move against him.

"Oh, Cara," he murmured against her lips. "Cara." And his husky caress incited her further. She was on fire everywhere she touched him, and that was everywhere that mattered. Her breasts were aching against his hairy chest. Her hips were undulating urgently against his, stirring him to greater passion. Her tender thighs pressed against his muscled ones.

At last he drew her legs up on either side of him, and Cara tossed back her head in surprise when he entered her, filling her with the awesome and thrilling power of him as he eased deeply into her softness.

"Oh, Cara," he said with a groan, and a fresh rush of

125

delight spiraled up her body, causing her skin to blush with heat. He was moving gently, rocking against her body, his hands on her hips controlling their movements.

Cara thought she would surely die from the exquisite pleasure he was giving her. Slowly, erotically, maddeningly, he eased her up and down on his body, sending rivers of thrills deep into the most vulnerable and tender parts of her body.

Leaning over his chest, she kissed him, her tongue easing inside his mouth to meet his. The kiss deepened, and Jud increased the pace of their passion. Cara's desire was so strong that she didn't know if she could stand the dizzying heights Jud was taking her to. She felt overwhelmed by her need, lost in a sea of rapture, eager to touch the shores of final ecstasy. She was sure she couldn't wait for Jud if he didn't soon free her from the sensual waves of pleasure washing up inside her, battering at her senses until she thought she would drown in her desire.

A fine sheen of perspiration coated her body, causing it to glow softly in the golden light of the moon. Cara opened her mouth and silently moaned in delicious agony as she rode the swells of Jud's passion, going higher and higher with each passing second.

"Now, Cara, now," Jud murmured urgently, his voice passion thick. He arched his body a final time to thrust into Cara's, and she cried out her joy to the night.

For a long time she stayed astride Jud, her eyes closed, her head back, her face to the moon, not wanting to break the magic of the mood. Her body tingled in the aftermath of desire, and her heart cried out its delight. Wrapped in the splendor of Jud's loving, she felt whole as never before.

Thoughts eventually began to surface, hopefully, daringly. Was it too soon to believe that she could love again? When Jud had told her to live life fully, to go out and fall in love, had he meant with him?

She slowly opened her eyes and gazed down at him. He was watching her with a dazed expression in his dark eyes.

Surely he had felt it, too—had known that what had just happened between them was something special, something that didn't happen every day.

She told herself that if she could believe in ESP, if she could be sure that there was knowledge beyond what was seen and touched and heard, then it could also be true that she and Jud had been destined for each other. Or was she only grasping at straws now? Was she so enamored of him, so in love—for want of another word—after this incredible experience that she wanted to convince herself that he cared for her, too?

His fingers began to play over her breasts gently, caressingly, and Cara shivered.

"Are you cold?" he murmured.

"No," she whispered. The temperature was still in the seventies, and even if it weren't, the heat from his body and her own was enough to start a blaze.

"I'm sure not," he murmured. "I can't recall when I've burned so, Cara. Is that some trick, some black magic that only you psychologists know about—the way you set a man on fire? Lord, woman, I thought I was going to be consumed by the flames."

Laughing softly, Cara traced the cleft in his chin with a trembling fingertip. Hadn't she thought the same thing?

"I don't know if I'll ever cool off," he whispered thickly. "I don't know if I want to."

With his body still united with Cara's, he eased her over on her back and began to kiss her again. She didn't know if she could survive more of his loving, but with everything in her, she was willing to try.

127

CHAPTER EIGHT

Later, after she had again crested love's most erotic peaks, Cara lay cradled in Jud's arms on the soft grass, listening to his breathing as it became regular again.

"When I spoke of love being a voyage of discovery," he murmured, "I was thinking of the mind. I like voyages of the body better. Discovering yours was a rare pleasure, lady."

"You weren't so bad yourself," she whispered. The pleasure she had experienced had been incomparable.

Jud locked his fingers in her hair and lifted her head so that he could claim her mouth again, then he freed her. "If I don't cool off before I go back to the house, I'll sear the sheets," he said in a thick voice.

Cara laughed gently. "Those black sheets of yours look durable enough."

"Will you come and sleep with me on them?"

Although Cara wanted that more than anything in the world, she immediately shook her head. She was afraid Justin would somehow find out, and she didn't want him to know what had happened until she had a chance to talk with him.

"No," she made herself say.

"Why not?"

She hesitated, and she could feel Jud begin to withdraw from her. "I—I just don't think it's proper," she stammered.

"But this is?" he asked with the faintest trace of sarcasm.

"That's not what I meant to imply at all," she retorted, stung by his response. "It's just that I came with Justin and—"

"And what?" he interrupted rudely. He didn't want to, but he was doubting her assertion that she hadn't slept with Justin. She had some close tie to him, some involvement with him. That was plain enough to see.

Cara could feel the exquisite joy they had just shared evaporating, and she couldn't bear for that to happen. She had to make Jud realize how she felt about Justin. Surely he was sensitive enough to understand that under the circumstances, she didn't want to flaunt her romance with him right under Justin's nose. Or was he so bitter when it came to Justin that he would do anything to hurt him? The question sent a shudder through her body, and she wouldn't explore it further.

"He's been good to me," she said fervently. "He's been a tremendous help with my book. I feel a deep loyalty to him. And anyway," she said lightly, "he brought me here to you."

Jud didn't want to fall for her line, but he had already fallen for *her*. He didn't want to shatter the special experience they had just shared by bickering about Justin, of all people. He had promised himself that he would live his life and leave Justin to do the same, as long as their two paths didn't cross. But he had been the one to invite Justin here—and with him had come this treasure.

"Let's go take a swim in the pond," Jud said unexpectedly, rising to his feet and drawing Cara to hers.

"You're not serious," she cried, the idea sounding terribly wicked.

"Of course I am," he returned. "Have you ever gone skinny-dipping at night?"

"Not at night or in the daytime either. It sounds positively decadent!"

"Good," he said, hugging her naked form to his. "I was

just telling myself when I saw you yesterday that that was exactly what you needed—some decadence in your life. Come on," he coaxed. "You'll love it."

Before she could protest further, he lifted her in his arms and raced down to the water's edge with her. Still carrying her, he waded into the pond. The water was chilly, and Cara's nipple tightened where it pressed against Jud's chest. After a while he released her, letting her body slide down his.

"I hope that's me causing that reaction in you and not the cold water," he whispered, holding her to him.

Cara moaned softly as her body again molded to his. If it had been the chilly water, it wasn't now. In fact, she was surprised the water didn't turn to steam, so hot was she.

"What kind of creatures swim around in here?" she asked breathlessly, ashamed of her desire for him and wanting to focus on something else.

Jud laughed. "Nothing that will hurt you, I assure you. Would I let that happen?"

"Oh, God, I hope not," she said softly, and the statement carried a wealth of meaning.

Jud's mouth found her ear to stroke it gently with his tongue, sending a shiver over Cara's body. "Has something hurt you, little girl?" he whispered. "Is that why you hide behind your glasses and your profession?"

For a brief insane moment Cara wanted to let her defenses down and tell him all about Lance and how he had gone with her for three years, then married the college homecoming queen. But it seemed so far in the past now, and it seemed an absurd thing to confess to a naked man holding her in a pond enchantingly golden from the yellow light of the moon.

Cara smiled at the ridiculousness of it all. "I don't tell secrets to naked men who are all wet," she said with a laugh in her voice.

Abruptly Jud swept her off her feet, only to toss her into

the water. "Jud!" she cried, flailing madly, but then she found that the bottom was solid under her feet, and she realized that the water was little more than waist deep where they stood.

"Yes, my little mind explorer. Is there something I can do for you? Better still," he whispered wickedly, "is there something I can do *to* you?"

He pulled her to him and tried to kiss her, but Cara splashed water on him.

"Cad!" she cried. "Dumping me like that. I was scared to death!"

Suddenly Jud vanished. Cara looked all around, but the dark water had absorbed him, and even the moon couldn't shed any light on his whereabouts.

When she felt a bite on her bottom, she gasped. Unexpectedly Jud emerged right beside her.

"Woman-eating shark!" he declared. "Did you see it?"

"See it!" she exclaimed, going along with the game. "I felt it. It bit me."

"No fooling? Damned smart fish, I'd say. I think I'll try that. Lady, I could gobble you alive myself, in case you don't know it."

"Jud," she cried, before he could go under a second time. "Don't bite me again."

When he disappeared in spite of her protests, Cara began to swim away from him. She was fleeing, lost in laughter when Jud emerged behind her. She saw the water run off his muscled shoulders like liquid gold in the bright moonlight, and when he spied her he began to swim toward her.

Cara had seen an anchored raft in the center of the pond earlier, and she headed toward it with all her strength. She was determined to get away from Jud, but no matter how rapidly she stroked through the water, he gained on her. His long arms seemed to move effortlessly, and she stopped laughing to concentrate on the task of outracing him.

She had almost reached the ladder leading up to the platform when Jud submerged and grabbed her ankle. She let out a cry of protest as he dragged her under, and she was relieved to feel his strong arms around her as they both fought their way back to the top.

"Fiend!" she gasped as they broke the surface. "Taking advantage of helpless females."

Drawing her with him, Jud caught hold of the ladder. Cara grasped the slender bars with Jud's assistance, and just when she thought she had climbed to the safety of the raft, he hauled himself up on top and grabbed her again.

Cara hadn't expected it and she let out a howl of laughter as she collapsed on the planks. Jud stretched out on his side near her, laughing deeply.

When Cara shook out her long hair, then lay down on her back, Jud leaned over her. "You're so tempting, water nymph," he murmured. "So shapely and lovely with the moonlight spilling down on your wet body." He began to kiss away the drops of water that clung to her breasts, and Cara placed her hands on both sides of his face so that he would look at her.

"Don't you think we'd better get back, Jud?" she murmured. She had made love with him twice on the grass, and though she could understand his hunger because it matched her own, she was beginning to feel guilty about Justin. Surely he had missed them by now and was wondering where they were.

Jud studied her features for a moment, then snapped his fingers as he looked down at the luminous hands of his watch. Cara smiled at the incongruity of him being naked but still wearing his watch. When he saw her smile, he grinned.

"In all my excitement I forgot to take it off. Fortunately it's waterproof." He frowned. "I forgot all about Raymond, too. I'm supposed to talk to him about that stallion tonight."

Now that she had mentioned it, Cara was reluctant to go back, but she knew they had to eventually. She found herself wondering if she would ever see Jud again. He hadn't even hinted at that, and her spirits suddenly began to sink. She knew he was leaving soon to buy the stallion.

"Well, don't lie there wasting time, woman," he joked, seeing her hesitation. "Let's take the plunge."

Cara stood up, and before Jud even knew what she was doing, she had indeed plunged over the side.

"Wait, Cara!" he called, concern in his voice. "You don't know this pond."

He jumped off the raft in pursuit of her, but Cara had waited, and when he emerged, shook his hair out of his eyes and looked all around for her, she dived beneath the water and jerked him down by one leg.

"Witch," he declared in a stern voice that barely concealed his laughter when they both rose to the surface.

Delighted to have finally paid him in kind, Cara smiled. Then they set out for the shore, swimming side by side.

She was subdued as he led her back to where they had left their clothes, and neither of them said anything as they dressed. Hand in hand they made their way back toward the lights of the house. When they were a short distance from it, Cara turned to Jud.

"You don't have to walk me to my door," she said, trying to make a joke and not succeeding very well.

Jud stared at her for a moment, then nodded. "All right. You get some sleep." He glanced down at his watch. "It's after ten and I told Raymond I needed to talk to him tonight. I have to leave early tomorrow morning to drive to Texas."

"I see," she murmured. Was he going to leave her without saying any more than that? No mention of seeing her again sometime?

She gazed into his dark eyes, and when he said nothing more, she murmured thickly, "Good night." Then she turned away and hurried the short distance to the front porch.

133

She didn't glance back at Jud's retreating back until she had gone up the steps. Her arms around one of the tall columns, she gazed after her lover and wondered if she'd just made an absolute fool of herself.

The porch light was off, and when a dark figure stepped out of the shadows, Cara drew in her breath sharply. As the figure moved closer, the hall light spilling out through the screen door revealed Justin's tall form, and Cara sighed in relief. The relief, however, was short-lived when she saw the condemning expression on his face.

"Did you make love with Jud down by the pond?" he demanded, his voice full of bitterness.

Cara's mouth was still open. Had he seen them? How did he know that?

"You did!" he accused scornfully when shock and embarrassment made it impossible for her to respond. "And after all that garbage you gave me about not getting involved with your subjects! What a crock! Well, you've just been *used*, lady, in case you don't know it. You should have taken your own advice and stayed out of brother dear's arms."

"You don't know what you're talking about," Cara cried, but she could say little in defense of herself. She had behaved badly, making love with Jud under the circumstances.

"The hell I don't!" he countered. He laughed mirthlessly. "I made love to Brenda, Jud's fiancée, down by the pond, too. That's why he took you there. It was after a party just like the barbecue tonight. The man's just used you, made a royal fool of you, Cara, and you let him do it. A fine psychologist you are! You can't handle yourself. How do you expect to handle anyone else?"

Cara sucked in her breath at his words. *Justin had made love to Jud's fiancée down by the pond.* She almost couldn't believe what she was hearing. No wonder there was such animosity between them.

And although Justin was speaking in anger, that fact

didn't downplay the importance of what he was saying—or the folly of what she had done.

Pieces of a puzzle she hadn't wanted to see began to fall into place. Hadn't Jud repeatedly and insistently demanded to know if she had made love with Justin? He had seemed obsessed by the fact, and though she had denied it, maybe he hadn't believed her. Maybe Justin knew exactly what he was talking about.

As his blazing eyes bored into her, Cara was shaken to the core. She felt just like the fool Justin had accused her of being. How could she have been so stupid? She who so smugly told herself that she was skilled in the ways of the mind had been outmaneuvered by an amateur. Jud had taken her to the pond and made love to her where his brother had made love to his fiancée. He had gotten his revenge and made a mockery of her and her project all in one clean sweep.

Shame flooded through her; she was a poor excuse for a psychologist, she told herself. It was a good thing she was doing a book, for she was learning some necessary lessons from the research. Jud was right: she did need to live, to explore herself. Jud had used her—so cleverly. And so cruelly. Because of that she was looking inside and she didn't like what she saw. What a bitter lesson to learn.

Somehow she had to salvage some of her pride. She had been enough of a fool already tonight; she would not permit herself to fall apart in front of Justin. She raised her chin as high as her damaged pride would permit and spoke in a firm voice.

"If I've made myself look bad in your eyes, I'm sorry. Those things happen. But just because I was attracted to your brother doesn't mean that he used me or that I'm an inept psychologist. My personal life has nothing to do with the way I handle other people's problems. I can still be objective and effective."

She told herself that she should have received an academy

135

award for that bit of lies and rhetoric, but it had given her enough courage to turn away from him and walk to the front door. Justin might think she had been fool enough to make love with Jud, but she hadn't admitted that she had gone that far.

She wanted desperately to grab her suitcase and flee forever from these two brothers, but she knew that right now wasn't the moment. She would have to get through the night as best she could, then escape in the morning.

Hearing Justin's angry footsteps as he followed her inside, Cara waited until she again thought she could speak calmly before she looked back at him. His fury was revealed by the tense lines around his mouth, and his accusing dark eyes.

"I really need to leave early in the morning, Justin. Do you mind if we skip breakfast?"

"The sooner we leave, the better," he said coldly. "I don't want to see my brother's face again—ever."

That makes two of us, she told herself miserably. She thought derisively that she had accomplished one hell of a lot here in two days. Not only had she managed to widen the gap between the brothers, she had succeeded in doing enough damage to herself to last a lifetime.

Swallowing the lump forming in her throat, she made herself speak rationally. "Good. Shall we say five-thirty then?"

Justin looked at her strangely for a moment, and she could see the indecision in his eyes. She was praying that her unexpected desire to leave had thrown him off the track. After all, would a woman who had just made love to a man want to skip out before she even saw him again?

Cara didn't care what he thought as long as he got her out of here before she had to see Jud. She had thought she had been hurt before, but this was pain and humiliation as she had never imagined it.

Less than half an hour ago she had been dreaming stupid dreams of love. Love! She could hardly believe it! What an utter fool she had been! She deserved everything Justin had said and more! For he didn't know the half of it.

Jud had used her own techniques to outwit her, to make her see logic that was misdirected. He had analyzed her, properly diagnosed her and exploited her for his own purposes. And she had gone into his arms so fast that it had probably made his head spin. She wanted to scream out her misery and shame, to shout it to the hills and beyond. She wanted to tell Justin just how right he was. She wanted to vent her anger at Jud's betrayal, but instead, with incredible calm and dignity, she looked into Justin's dark eyes and said, "Good night, Justin. I'll see you in the morning." Then she opened the door and took step after torturous step into Jud's house until she had walked down the hall. For a shameful moment she stood outside his room, gazing into its darkness. Hours ago she had imagined herself there making love with Jud. Minutes ago he had invited her to share that bed with him.

She smiled grimly. Surely he had had his excuse about seeing Raymond ready even then. He had achieved his aim; he didn't need to sleep with her again. Twice by the pond had been enough. What was it he had told her the first time he had kissed her—with twins you get twice the loving? Well, now she had had twice the loving with one twin, and, like Justin, she never wanted to see that twin's face again.

The irony of his words came back to haunt her. Had he known, planned, even while he was saying those things to her that he would somehow get her out to the pond and claim her? Well, she had made it all so easy for him, hadn't she? She had fallen right into his scheme—and his arms. And yes, she could most certainly write about her erotic fantasies with him now. He had fulfilled every dream, every conceivable imaginary moment of wondrous love.

She laughed aloud self-mockingly, but the laughter quickly died on her lips and her eyes filled with tears. They began to tumble down her cheeks as she stripped off the shorts and top Jud had so recently and thrillingly taken from her body. Naked, tears streaming, Cara climbed under the silk sheet, turned her face toward the pillow and sobbed until she was shaking uncontrollably.

How she got through the night Cara never knew. She heard Jud come in about an hour after she had gone to bed, and she listened, filled with mortification, as he made his way down the hall, entered his room and finally went to bed. The house became quiet and still, but Cara was afraid to fall asleep, even if it had been possible. She had to get out of there before Jud got up.

She was sure she dozed a couple of times, but each time she awakened with a start, looked at the clock, then closed her tired eyes again. When five o'clock dragged around she crept from the bed, threw on some slacks and a top, shoved her other clothes into the suitcase, then went to the bathroom.

The face in the mirror shocked her, but she should have expected no less after her weeping spell and tormented night. She quietly splashed cold water on her face and puffy lids, then discreetly hid the worst of the rings under her eyes with a creamy cover-up. She practiced a smile for Justin, but it was useless.

Her suitcase in hand, she silently crept down the hall and up the stairs. She could hear her own breathing, wild and fast, in her ears as she lightly tapped on Justin's door. He opened it immediately.

In contrast to Cara's weary appearance, this morning Justin seemed fresh as a daisy. But then she had never seen him when he wasn't bandbox perfect no matter what the circumstances. He was looking sheepish and apologetic, and she just prayed he would save it all until they got out to the car.

"Ready to go?" she murmured. "I'm really in a hurry."

He looked at her curiously, but he nodded. "Yes. Just let me get my suitcase."

She watched as he made his way across the room and picked up the luggage from the bed. He was smiling at her when he returned, but she was thankful that he remained quiet until they had slipped down the steps and out the front door. Not a soul had stirred. Cara had escaped. But it didn't bring her any pleasure.

After Justin started the car and they drove away, he glanced over at her. "I'm afraid I behaved very badly last night." He smiled, and Cara realized he was trying valiantly to be his old charming self once more now that he was away from his brother's house. His gaze returned to the road.

"I got a little crazy when I saw you and Jud coming back from the direction of the pond, holding hands. Both of you looked as though you had taken a dip, but your clothes were barely damp. I jumped to conclusions. Now, I don't blame you for what you did," he rushed on. "I know how he is with the ladies, and I just assumed—well, I imagined that he had made love to you to get even with me."

Cara could feel his gaze on her again. "I'm sorry," he murmured. "I didn't mean to insult you."

"I want to explain about Brenda," he said, his eyes burning as he looked at her. "I don't want you to think the worst of me." He licked his lips, then continued before Cara could stop him. "It was just one of those things that happens. It was at a party Jud gave, and we'd both had too much to drink. People were making twin jokes—you know, the kind about how she probably didn't even know which brother she was marrying and couldn't tell us apart."

"Justin," Cara murmured. "You don't need to tell me this." In fact, she would rather not hear it.

"But I want to," he said sincerely. "Brenda was in a brief blue bikini. She was so appealing—so sexy." He shrugged. "It just happened. Can you understand that?"

Cara told herself that she could *almost* understand it, but not quite. Not the woman his brother had intended to make his wife. But she offered no comment. She was too confused herself to be someone else's judge.

"It didn't mean anything, really," Justin stressed. "But Brenda admitted it to Judson. I was remembering it all when you two returned. That's why I got so upset."

Cara wanted desperately to lie, to save her self-respect, to let Justin believe he had overreacted. But she wasn't that kind. She did feel that she owed him the truth, for whatever reasons. Just like Brenda, she told herself bitterly, she had to put the painful facts right up front.

She met his gaze, then glanced off at the wildflowers blowing in the light breeze at the side of the road. "We did make love down at the pond."

When she looked at him again, she saw his hands tighten on the wheel and his jaw muscles twitch convulsively. "Justin," she murmured quietly, "I never meant to hurt you or in any way be disloyal to you. You've been my friend. It was just that"—she couldn't meet his eyes—"that I was so physically attracted to Jud that I weakened. I didn't mean to get involved with my subjects," she hurried on, for it had been true. She had seen the folly of doing that.

When he uttered an expletive, Cara turned to him. "Surely you of all people can understand how it happens, Justin. You . . ." Her words trailed off. Incredibly, she had been about to attempt to excuse her own actions, to make them look less distasteful, by reminding him of how he had made love with Brenda.

Biting her lip to stop a fresh surge of tears, she shook her head and stared out the window. What a confused mess this had all turned out to be. Well, she told herself bitterly, she had wanted to research twins. And she had most certainly done that. She had had enough of twins to last her a lifetime. When her book was finished, she didn't ever want to think double anything!

Justin stomped on the accelerator again, whipping the car around the twisting road with dangerous speed. Cara refused to show fear; sitting with her hands clasped tightly in her lap, she endured the mad ride. At last it ended and, miraculously, she was delivered to her house still in one piece.

To her chagrin, she saw old Mrs. Drexler out in her flower garden, snipping roses. She turned around, alarmed when the car screeched to a halt, but when she saw Justin, her features relaxed.

"Good morning, Mr. Garrett," she said warmly, her wrinkled face breaking into a big smile, her green eyes lighting up.

To Cara's astonishment, Justin flashed her a big smile. But he didn't speak to Cara. Her purse and briefcase in hand, she opened the door and started around the car to get her luggage.

Justin climbed out and quickly went to the back to set Cara's suitcase on the curb. "How are you this morning, Mrs. Drexler?" he asked, smiling at the old woman as he deliberately ignored his companion.

"Fine. Just fine."

"I'm glad to hear it." Without another word Justin climbed back into the car, started it with a clashing of gears and roared off.

For a moment Cara stared after him, wishing he didn't hate her so much.

She was startled when Mrs. Drexler addressed her. "Did you take a trip, Cara?"

Refusing to let her pry, Cara nodded. "Yes, and it went just swimmingly." If she had had the heart, she would have laughed at her own pun. But she didn't. Wearily she made her way up the steps to her rooms. More than anything in the world she wanted to go back home.

CHAPTER NINE

As the days passed Cara stopped berating herself for having gotten involved with Jud. She concentrated solely on her project. She was at the critical point now. All her research had been done, and she had written most of the book. Thank God for the computer she had been able to lease for three months, she told herself. Without it she didn't know how she would have managed. She would type up pages, print them out, go home and pore over them endlessly, editing until she was satisfied.

She didn't hear a word from Jud, but then she hadn't expected to. He had done what he wanted with her; still, every time the phone rang she imagined that it was he. When Justin called toward the end of the week, pleading to see her, she explained firmly that she had to work. She didn't want any more emotional upsets—for either of them.

When she did work in her office, she was apparently fortunate enough to miss Justin if he came looking for her. She knew it was better for both of them if she just kept working and tried to forget the brothers. And yet as she worked, she knew some of her most revealing facts had come from those two men. She was grateful that at least her work had benefited.

A week passed before Cara had any contact with anyone. By the time Saturday morning finally dragged around, she simply had to take a break from her routine. She had seen Mrs. Drexler down in her garden tending to her flowers, and she joined her just to hear the sound of another human voice.

"You've been awfully quiet up there in your rooms," the old woman said, bending over a lovely yellow rosebush to snip off the dead blossoms. "I've hardly heard a peep out of you. How's the book going?"

"Better than I had hoped," Cara admitted. She reached out to caress a beautiful white rosebud. "I may be able to leave next week."

"Then I'll be needing to put a notice in the paper for a new tenant," the old woman said, pausing in her pruning. "I'm sure you won't mind me showing the rooms if someone's interested before you move out." Her voice was sharp. "I need to rent those rooms to get by, what with social security being what it is these days."

"I understand," Cara said.

The woman smiled and became cheerful again as she went back to her cutting. "Where's that nice Mr. Garrett? I haven't seen him all week. Has he been away?"

Immediately thinking of Jud, Cara almost said he had gone to Texas to buy a horse, but she realized her error in time. "I'm not sure. He's been busy, too, I think."

A car came around the corner, and Mrs. Drexler, who didn't miss a thing, glanced over her shoulder. The car slowed and the old woman asked, "Why, isn't that his car?"

Cara glanced in the direction of the vehicle. It was Justin, and she sighed unhappily as he parked.

"Yoo-hoo, Mr. Garrett," Mrs. Drexler called out in a merry voice. "Good morning."

Cara fought down a flood of memories as she watched Justin. He had been so angry the last time she had seen him, and she was sorry that he had come now. It was impossible not to think of Jud as his twin stood before her, and she just wanted to be left alone to finish her book and go home. But she couldn't very well run away now. A sudden memory of Jud accusing her of always running rushed to her mind, and she pursed her lips as though that would help suppress any unwanted thoughts.

Hastily climbing out of the car, Justin managed a quick smile for Mrs. Drexler, but his dark gaze was on Cara. "Good morning," he said to the young woman. "I was hoping I'd find you at home."

"Good morning," she returned resignedly.

"I thought I might take you to breakfast at the café." Justin's tone was more hopeful than it was bold.

Cara glanced at the old woman, who stood with pruning shears in hand, unabashedly watching the young couple. When she looked back at Justin, it was on the tip of her tongue to tell him that he knew she was too busy with her book. But she realized they needed to clear the air between them.

"All right," she murmured. "I'll go get my purse."

Justin winked at her. "That's my girl."

As she walked away Cara heard the old woman murmuring something about the sweetness of young love. She wanted to turn around and tell her how wrong she was. But of course she didn't.

She freshened her makeup, picked up her purse and returned. Justin opened the car door for her, and Cara slid inside. She watched as he climbed in the driver's side, then waited for him to initiate the conversation. He was the one with things to say, after all.

"Thanks for coming with me," he said, gazing at her as he started the car. "I've been trying to reach you, but it didn't take a genius to figure out that you didn't want to see me again."

"I thought it best," she said resignedly.

Justin pulled out into traffic, then said softly, "Don't hate me, Cara. I'm sorry I blew up like that." He shook his head. "That's twice now I've apologized for my temper, and believe it or not, I don't usually find myself in that position."

144

He forced a smile. "You and Jud seem to bring out the worst in me."

He glanced at her, then back at the road. "I don't suppose you've heard anything from Jud."

"No, I haven't," she said in a barely controlled voice. "Is that why you asked me out—to find out what's going on with Jud and me?"

Immediately he directed the car to the curb and stopped it. "No, it's not. Please don't start out by being defensive and angry. I want to be your friend. That is possible, isn't it?"

Since she had met Jud, it seemed to Cara that she had been in a constant state of turmoil. She was more embarrassed than she could admit. She was defensive and angry— angry at the wrong person. Shaking her head, she admitted to herself that only Jud and Justin had the power to make her so angry and defensive.

"I'm sorry," she said, looking down at her nails, then back at Justin. She and he had been friends before she ever met Jud, and in spite of Justin trying to court her—perhaps because of it—she had liked him immensely. "You and Jud seem to bring out the worst in *me,*" she said, trying to inject a teasing tone in her voice.

She drew in a steadying breath, then continued. "I would like to be your friend," she said frankly. "I've always liked you, Justin, and I will never forget that you helped me feel at home here. When I didn't know anyone, you made me welcome. You introduced me to people. I owe you a lot for that, and I won't forget it."

"I hope you'll be my friend not because you think you owe me something but because you like me," he said with the hint of a grin. "Who knows? One day you might be a really successful writer or psychologist and I can point to you and say, 'Hey, she's my friend.'"

Cara laughed for the first time in days. "Oh, the old 'I like you for who you are, not what you are' game," she said jokingly. "Well, I hate to disappoint you, but celebrity status isn't in the cards for me. Anyway, in less than two weeks I'll be going home. You won't even remember my name, much less hear of me being famous."

"I'll remember your name," he said gently. "Call it that ESP you're always talking about if you will, but I think you and I will always be friends—special friends."

"I'd like to believe that," she murmured.

Justin nodded. "Me, too." Then he drove away from the curb and headed to the café.

Cara loved the familiar feel of the place, and Justin couldn't have chosen a better spot to renew their friendship. In the calm and warm atmosphere they began to talk openly and honestly with each other. Cara hadn't wanted the tension between them, and she hadn't wanted him to think the worst of her any more than he had wanted her to think it of him.

"You really care for Jud, don't you?" he murmured in surprise as she tried to explain how she had wound up in his brother's arms.

She could feel the tears well up in her eyes, but she tried to joke. "Don't call me a fool again," she said with a bitter laugh. "We just got over that part."

Reaching out to pat her hand, Justin said softly, "I won't. I'm glad to hear that it wasn't a step you took lightly." Now it was his turn to laugh. "It hurt my manly ego to think you'd let him make love to you while you kept brushing me off."

Cara wrapped her hands around her iced tea glass. "I never meant for it to happen with Jud. I've never been able to separate caring and sex, I guess." She glanced up at him. "It's a big failing of mine." Her gold-brown eyes held his. "I hear it's a big failing of yours, too—in the opposite direction."

"What do you mean?" he said, but Cara noticed that his expression wasn't all innocence.

"I mean you can't sleep with a dozen women and think each time it's love."

"Here it comes," Justin said, and his laughter was slightly embarrassed. "I'm going to get a free hour of psychoanalysis."

"We're friends, right?" she asked, her gaze still holding his.

Justin nodded. "At least I'm not going to have to pay for this."

Cara squeezed his hand. "You're a wonderful, sensitive, handsome man, Justin. Don't throw yourself away on dozens of women. Find one you love and who will love you, and make a commitment." She glanced away. "Take some advice from an old pro. Go out and fall in love."

She didn't tell him the old pro was his brother, and when he looked at her questioningly, she smiled. "Something I learned along the way."

"And you took the advice, huh?" he asked.

Knowing he was talking about Jud, she nodded ruefully.

"Then take your own advice," he murmured. "Don't throw yourself away on a man like him. Find one who will love you."

Cara gave him a playful salute. "You learn very quickly for an amateur."

"That'll be fifty dollars," he said, holding out his hand.

Both of them laughed, but Cara's laughter didn't linger. Her thoughts were elsewhere. "What happened to Brenda?" she asked quietly, unable to help herself.

Justin sighed. "Ah, Brenda. I wish I'd never heard that name." He glanced around the café, then looked back at Cara. "Never one to let the grass grow under her feet, our girl Brenda promptly found another man when Jud dumped her. In fact, I'm sure she's found several by now, but one of them married her. They live about two hours up the road. She still comes around occasionally."

"I see."

147

"Cara," he said, effectively changing the subject, "about that party next Saturday night. You kind of said you'd go with me. Will you?"

She started to shake her head. She had only said she would think about it, but before she could say no, Justin murmured, "It will be good for your book. You've got to think about publicity."

"All right," she said, smiling again. But she didn't agree because of the book. She knew she couldn't hide herself away forever. Besides, Justin really was charming when he wanted to be. And she had enjoyed this outing with him immensely. It had already done wonders for her; she did feel like she had had a session with a psychologist. She had needed to talk to someone about Jud. She just hadn't expected it to be Justin. Her outing with him was almost like old times. Almost.

By the time the morning ended and Justin had driven her back to her place, she was ready to get back to work. She had needed the break, and she had needed to talk. Now she could work better. She spent the rest of the day polishing her book, then took a long bath and went to bed early. She wanted to be fresh for the next morning. If she worked hard all week, she thought she could finish the book. Then all that would be left would be to go home. She would leave her Virginia memories right here when she got on that plane to California.

By seven o'clock Sunday morning Cara was in her office doing cleanup work on the book. She left her door open, since no one else was expected on a Sunday. All the occupants of the building had a front door key as well as an office key, so she wasn't worried about anyone coming in who didn't belong there.

She had only been working about fifteen minutes when she heard someone opening the main door. Her office was right down the hall on the first floor. Briefly she puzzled over who would be coming in, then decided it was someone like herself, with work that couldn't wait. She got up, shut her door and went back to typing.

A moment later she looked up in surprise when someone rapped twice, then opened the door. She adjusted her glasses on her nose and stared at the intruder in surprise.

"Jud!" she exclaimed. "What are you doing here?" She could feel that familiar rapid beating of her heart at the sight of him, and her skin was warm and flushed.

"Aren't I welcome?" he asked with a smile.

Welcome, she repeated incredulously to herself. She couldn't believe his gall.

"Actually, no!" she declared sharply. He was the last person in the world she wanted to see.

He came in, shut the door, then leaned back against it, his booted feet wide apart, his arms crossed over his chest. Cara's eyes raced over him, from his dark hair down his blue shirt and close-fitting jeans to his booted feet. The very sight of him unsettled her. She could feel herself becoming defensive and angry.

"And why's that?" he asked in response to her comment.

Cara took off her glasses and unconsciously began biting on the earpiece. When she realized what she was doing, she slammed them down on her desk.

"Who do you think you are?" she demanded at last. "Do you think you can waltz in and out of my life, toying with me as though I were your newest game?"

"Me?" he said in a low, angry voice. "You're a little confused, aren't you? What happened? The last I heard from you, you were still a guest in my house. When I went to breakfast the next morning, you and my little brother had departed."

"Well, what did you expect?" she flung at him.

He arched dark brows, then studied her from cold, dark eyes, his gaze going over her flushed features and shapely figure.

"At the moment I'm not real sure. A simple thank-you for

the weekend? Or did you think you had thanked me out at the pond?" he asked sharply. "Was that it?"

Cara could feel the blood surge to her cheeks. "Didn't you think I had? Wasn't that all you wanted? To get your revenge against Justin by making love to me there just as he had done with Brenda?"

She watched, astonished, as the blood drained from Jud's cheeks, leaving his handsome features stark and strained. He clenched his fists until they, too, were white and cruel-looking. Cara wasn't sure he didn't want to strike her.

"Is that what you think?" he demanded, his words sharp and cutting.

"What else am I to think?" she cried. "Isn't that what happened? Did you use me to get back at your brother because you knew he was interested in me?"

Jud stood there and stared at her for a minute, unable to believe what she had just said. He had been furious when he woke up and found that she had gone without so much as a by-your-leave, but this was too much.

He had suspected that Justin was behind her abrupt departure, and now she had confirmed it. But he was disgusted that she thought so little of him that she could believe he would stoop to such behavior.

"Did you work that out all by yourself, or did Justin help you? Frankly, I never knew *where* he made love to Brenda. Just knowing that he had was more than enough. If we chose the same place, perhaps it was more of that twin ESP you keep talking about. I'll just remind you that you were the one out at the pond—twice. You chose the place, not me."

His dark gaze flicked over her. "And you were the one who assured me there was nothing between you and Justin." His eyes burned into hers briefly, his lips twitching with suppressed anger. Then he turned on his heel, reached for the door and slammed out.

Cara stared blindly after him, not knowing what to think

or whom to believe. She felt like a ball being bounced back and forth by the battling brothers, first one angry with her, then the other.

But she realized all too plainly that this one was the one who really mattered to her. She was in love with Jud Garrett, for all the good it did her. She couldn't believe it, but it was true. And she wanted so desperately to believe that Justin had been wrong about him using her.

Jud had already stalked down the hall when Cara ran after him.

"Jud! Wait!" she called out.

He glanced back over his shoulder, and if looks could kill, she was sure she would be dead. He didn't slow down a single step, but when he reached the door and grabbed for it, he found he couldn't open it. For a moment he jiggled it so hard that Cara thought he would tear it from the frame.

"Hell," he said savagely, impotent with rage as he rattled the knob.

When he turned back to look at her, Cara was struck by the ridiculousness of the situation. It was plain to see that he hoped she never crossed his path again, but he was locked in and she was the one with the key.

"Open this damned door," he growled.

"The key's back in my office." She wanted to smile, but the situation was too critical.

Jud spun on his heel and strode angrily back in the other direction. Cara was surprised he hadn't attempted to kick the door down. She had never seen anyone so enraged. She wondered how he had gotten in and why he didn't know he couldn't get out again without a key.

"Who let you in?" she asked, following him into her office.

"The janitor. He's a friend of mine," he replied, his words clipped.

"How did you know I was here?"

Jud glared at her. "It sure wasn't through any fault of

yours. I wouldn't have asked Justin if my life depended on it, so I asked around town."

"Why did you come?"

There was a pregnant pause. The tension crackled in the air, and Cara was afraid Jud wasn't going to tell her.

"Why the hell do you think?" he finally muttered. "Because I *didn't* want to see you?"

Cara felt her hopes soar; maybe Justin had been wrong after all. Maybe they had both misread Jud. But she didn't want to be manipulated again. She must not jump to rash conclusions this time. "If you did, why didn't you call me?"

Jud ran his hands through his dark hair. "When? When you ran off at the break of day? Or during the week I was gone? Where? I had no phone number for you and you weren't listed."

Cara sighed in relief. At least he had tried. When she was alone in a strange town, she never listed the phone under her own name.

"Anyway," he said, his voice less harsh, "I thought I'd give you a little time to work out the facts for yourself. I had no way of knowing Justin would offer you a little tidbit about Brenda that even I didn't know."

And besides, he told himself, he had wanted the week to sort out his own feelings. He didn't quite trust this woman, and he hadn't been at all sure she wasn't playing a game with him, especially when she vanished so abruptly after giving herself to him.

He had tried to call her, but that was toward the end of the week, when he was on his way home. For the first time since Brenda, he was thinking about sharing his life with someone—and it was way too soon to think those thoughts, particularly with this woman who obviously had skeletons still rattling in her own romantic closet.

Cara didn't know what to say. Dare she be frank with him, trust herself with him again? She had acted imprudently when she gave herself to him. It had all happened too fast, but she had wanted him so. She would behave much more cautiously this time—if there was a this time.

Part of the problem, she knew, was that she thought she knew him so well—the touch of his mouth on hers, the caress of his fingers on her skin, the feel of his body as it joined with hers in rapturous union. Even mentally she had thought she knew him, for she had read all about his life on the questionnaires. She looked into his eyes, and there was no mistaking the agitation there, the confusion.

"I'm sorry I ran out like that," she told him. "I appreciate the time you spent with me."

He still stood there and stared at her, and Cara wished she could have bitten off her tongue. The statement sounded absurd under the circumstances, but what else could she have said. Thank you?

"Did you get the stallion?" she murmured at last, wondering why she hadn't thought of it sooner. It was neutral ground, something they could talk about civilly.

At first she thought Jud wasn't going to answer the question, but then she saw the glow begin in his brooding eyes. "Yes, I got him. You should see him. He's really something exceptional."

"I'd like to see him." She had blurted it out before she had thought about it.

"Would you?" he asked quietly. His eyes searched hers questioningly, and Cara prayed that he would extend an invitation.

"Do you want to come out to the ranch?"

"Yes, I'd like that."

He kept her in suspense for what seemed an eternity; then he nodded, as though he had made up his mind about something. "All right. After I take care of some other business in town, I'll take you out to see the horse."

"That would be wonderful," she said, as her heart began to soar. She had thought about Jud all week, no matter how foolish she told herself she was being, and she had longed to see him more than she would admit even to herself. She knew there were still many things to work out between them, and perhaps nothing would come of this attraction, but oh how she wanted to give it a chance to grow.

"The key," he murmured, holding out his hand.

Cara laughed gently. She had forgotten all about the key; she had been standing there staring at Jud, oblivious to all else. When she had retrieved it from her purse, she walked down the hall with him and opened the door.

"One o'clock?" he asked.

"Fine."

Unexpectedly he drew her to him and kissed her lips. Cara locked her arms around his neck and held him tightly to her. The kiss deepened, and Jud groaned as his hands moved low on her hips to crush her to his hard body.

She had missed him more than she would allow herself to admit, and now that she was back in his arms, it seemed so natural, so right. She wanted the moment to last forever; she didn't want to argue with him or think about the suspicions that had driven her from him. Her only desire was to love him and have him love her in return.

His mouth left hers to spill kisses down her slender throat, and she closed her eyes and parted her mouth, wanting more and more of him. A shiver raced over her as she remembered the heights he had taken her to when he had made love to her. She wanted that again—that wondrous feeling of touching the skies.

She heard someone clear his throat, and she opened her eyes to find one of the occupants of the building trying to brush past them. Embarrassed, Cara drew back from Jud.

"Pardon us," she murmured, barely glancing at the elderly man. She recognized him as a lawyer whose office was on the second floor.

He nodded brusquely, then quickly slipped around them and headed up the steps to the second floor. Jud waited until the man was out of hearing, then laughed softly.

"You're going to ruin my good name," he said hoarsely. "I don't want to get a reputation for seducing women in office buildings."

"I don't want that either," Cara said with mock sternness. "If it's only *one* woman, I wouldn't mind—but not women."

Jud laughed again, then lightly kissed her mouth. "One o'clock," he said, and vanished out the door.

Cara stood in the hall for a moment, wondering if she had imagined that he had come to her. She rubbed her arms, and when she felt how hot her flesh was, she knew that it hadn't been a dream. Only Jud could make her skin burn like that. Smiling to herself, she returned to her book, but she had to make herself concentrate. All she could think of was the handsome man who had just held her in his arms.

One o'clock didn't come too soon for her. She was eagerly awaiting Jud's return when she heard him rap on the outer door. She rushed down the hall with her key in hand.

"Hi," she said breathlessly, her eyes bright, her face glowing. If this wasn't love, she didn't know what was. But she wouldn't let herself think about that right now. She needed time. He needed time.

"Hi," he murmured. "Are you ready?"

"Yes." She didn't tell him she had been ready since he left. When she had picked up her purse, she walked with him out the door.

"It's a beautiful day, isn't it?" she asked, gazing up at the sunny sky as they walked to the car.

"Lovely," he agreed, but he was looking at her face, not at the sky.

CHAPTER TEN

"So," Jud said as they drove out to the ranch, "tell me why you kept running away from me. I find that I'm wild about you, and I need to know all I can to save myself."

His words made her tremble, and she was afraid he could see the quivers all the way to the ends of her fingertips. He turned toward her, and she looked deep into his eyes, wondering if she should tell all, be absolutely honest. Funny, but it didn't seem to matter now.

She mentally prepared the story in her mind, and for the first time she found that it didn't hurt to think about Lance Madison. "I met a man in college and fell in love," she said frankly. "Or at least I thought I was in love," she amended. She hadn't known what love was until this man came into her life, but she wasn't about to admit that so soon.

"I thought we would get married—not that he ever promised me that—but we dated for three years, and I trusted him implicitly. Then one day I blithely waltzed back onto the campus and heard that he had married the college beauty queen. Married, mind you! He had told me he was going home for the Easter holidays." She glanced away. "I guess he just didn't know how to tell me after all those years and the intimacy. So he didn't bother. It hurt like hell, I can tell you."

"What a bastard," he growled, taking his eyes off the road to look at her.

Cara smiled. "I got over it."

156

He reached over and squeezed her fingers. "I'm glad you did—and now that I think of it, I'm glad he married someone else." His expression was serious and caring. "I'm just sorry he hurt you."

She shrugged as if it were nothing. But she had cried for weeks after she found out, and every time she had passed Lance or his bride on the grounds of the school, she had felt physically sick.

"Now it's your turn. Tell me about Brenda." She really wanted to know everything, from how much he had loved her to how he felt about her now. To her chagrin, he answered it all in two statements.

"You've heard it all. There's nothing more to say."

Cara clenched her hands tightly in her lap. So he didn't want to talk about Brenda. Probably because he still cared about her.

"Jud, I—"

"I've been eager for you to see this stallion," he interrupted her, obviously trying to change the subject. "He's one of the most beautiful animals I've ever seen. His bloodline is impeccable. I consider myself lucky to have gotten him."

"I can't wait to see him," she said, putting a smile on her face. Nothing was to be gained by battering on closed doors at the moment. She would have to be very careful with him. He was a man thinking of the future, gingerly stepping into her world, but still tied to the past by his unresolved painful memories. Her gaze traveled over his handsome face. He was one of the most beautiful men she had ever seen, and like a spirited horse who had been spooked, he would have to be handled with care.

When he had parked the car, he reached over and drew Cara to him. "I've missed you terribly," he murmured. "I didn't want to let you out of my life. Thanks for coming back."

Smiling at him, she whispered, "The pleasure is all mine, I assure you."

He slid his fingers into her rich sable hair and lowered his head so that he could kiss her. Their lips met in a gentle, lingering caress, and when he drew away from her, his eyes were dark with passion.

"We'd better get out of here," he said thickly, "if you want to see anything besides me. When I touch you, my skin heats up all over and it must fog my brain, because I can't think of anything else but making love to you."

Cara laughed gently. Hadn't she said that to herself a dozen times about him?

"Don't laugh," Jud said. "I'm ready right now to let you lay me down on your psychologist's couch and explore me." He grinned. "All of me—outside first."

"Jud, you're impossible," she said, laughter in her voice.

He reached for her again. "Let me show you how impossible," he growled. "I want you, Cara. I dream about you day and night. I don't think I'll ever be able to get enough of you." His mouth found hers again, and his lips caressed hers passionately.

"Lord," he said huskily, thrusting her from him. "We'd better either go inside or go see that stallion. I don't want to get caught making love to you in the car. I haven't done that since I was sixteen."

Cara managed a tremulous smile, but a vision of him young and eager, with a pretty girl, rose in her mind. She didn't like it at all. "I've never made love in a car, and I don't intend to," she said primly, brushing at her hair.

Jud laughed deeply. "Woman, before I'm through with you, you're going to be doing lots of things you never even dreamed of."

"I doubt that," she said, feeling a shiver inside. But she had already done those things—making love under the moon's golden light at the pond, swimming in the black of night, naked. What else did he have in mind—and where would it lead?

Abruptly he grabbed her hand and pulled her out his side

of the car. "Let's go see the horse," she said breathlessly, not sure what he intended.

He wrapped his arm around her and began walking with her. "That's where we were headed," he said. "You weren't trying to run from me again, were you? I'm not Lance," he said softly. "I won't hurt you."

"Promise me," she said, pretending to tease, but she would give anything if he could make the promise and mean it. Was there room for her in a heart already crowded by Brenda and damaged by Justin?

"I promise you," he said solemnly. Then he embraced her. Her heart began to pound as he held her close. "I promise," he said again, his breath warm on her face.

Oh how Cara wanted to believe him, but she couldn't. Not yet. She would not make hasty judgments a second time.

The horse was housed over in the north pasture, so Jud saddled a couple of horses for himself and Cara, explaining that his stable boy had the weekend off.

"It must be nice to have people to do things for you," Cara commented, thinking of all the people who worked for him.

"Yes, and it's nice for them to have me to pay them, too," Jud said reasonably, and Cara smiled. She couldn't argue with that logic. She watched him as he worked, thinking how capable he was. He was a good boss, too, she recalled, remembering how fond Raymond and his family were of him. And she knew he treated Goldie as if she were family.

When her horse was ready, she swung up on the mare's back with an agility that surprised even her.

"You're a quick learner," Jud commented, grinning at her.

Cara laughed, but she recalled how badly she had failed when she first tried to ride with him. It had been a mere week ago, but it seemed like an eternity. How she had missed him during that time.

When they reached the pasture where the stallion was,

Cara climbed down off her mount and walked with Jud to the fence. The horse was magnificent. Black and shiny, he stood some distance from them and watched them warily, his body regal, his head held high.

Jud whistled for him, but he didn't come. His ears twitched and pricked up, but Jud hadn't yet succeeded in charming him. "He's arrogant," Jud commented with a grin, "but you wait, I'll have him eating out of my hand just like the ladies before too long."

Cara laughed. She knew he was talking about the mares taking sugar from him, but she understood all too well how easily he might have other females come at his beck and call.

He produced a lump of sugar and tried to coax the stallion forward with it, but the horse was having no part of strangers with gifts. "What does that mean, psychologist?" Jud asked, turning to Cara with a wicked look in his eyes. "Are the males smarter than the females, or is it the other way around?"

Smiling, Cara shook her head. "I guess it depends. If the females want the sugar and are bright enough to come and get it, then they're smarter than the male who wants it but is afraid."

Jud gazed at her thoughtfully for a moment, then nodded. "I see what you mean." Glancing back at the stallion, he tossed the sugar over the fence. When he turned back to Cara, he drew her into his arms.

"I want the sugar," he murmured thickly, "and I'm smart enough to go after it." His head descended, and he took gentle possession of her mouth.

"Sweeter than any honey," he said against her lips. His mouth left hers to trail down her neck, and Cara arched it to receive his warm kisses.

She had felt a sudden rush of desire the moment Jud touched her, and she knew she had to draw away before the flames became too hot. Pushing at his broad shoulders, she murmured, "This afternoon sun is burning me up, Jud." She wasn't lying; she was on fire, but it wasn't from the sun, despite its summer heat.

His dark eyes roamed over her flushed features for a moment, then he snapped his fingers. "I have a wonderful idea. Let's go up into the mountains where the air conditioning comes with the territory. It's beautiful there, and much cooler than here."

"I need to work on my book," she murmured halfheartedly, wanting more than anything to take off with him.

"It's Sunday," he said firmly. "Even *you* need some time off. Come on. If you've never traveled the Blue Ridge Highway, then you haven't seen the most beautiful country God ever made. A blue mist hangs over the Blue Ridge Mountains, but that's not the half of it. The vistas are grand, especially this time of year with the trees and flowers lush and gorgeous."

"I haven't seen the Blue Ridges, but I know about gray haze," Cara joked. "We call it smog in California."

"This is air you can breathe," Jud said with a smile. "Besides, there's a reunion of the Eaneses and the Garretts up there. I want you to meet the family. You'll love them— cousins, aunts, uncles, so many people you won't be able to remember them all."

"Oh?" Cara murmured, feeling a small thrill race over her because he wanted her to meet his relatives. Then she remembered the forgotten brother. "Will Justin be there?"

She could see the change in Jud at the mention of his brother's name, and she wanted to tell him how cruel and unreasonable he was being. But she had just reestablished her footing with him. Now wasn't the hour to talk about Justin.

"Justin doesn't go to these things," he answered. "They aren't sophisticated enough for a young lawyer. Maybe they aren't for a psychologist-writer, either."

Cara made herself smile. "Oh, I don't know. Perhaps I need the education. And who knows, I might run into more twins there, and even though it's too late for my book, the personal knowledge might be valuable."

"Then let's go," he said, a smile slowly curving his lips. "You'll love it, I promise. They'll have Brunswick stew, made with chicken, rabbit, squirrel and lots of home-grown vegetables."

"Rabbit and squirrel," Cara muttered, her lip curling in distaste at the thought.

"Come on, city girl," Jud coaxed. "There will be folk music with banjos, guitars, fiddles, harmonicas and foot stomping."

Cara was sorely tempted. One day wouldn't hurt; most of it was gone already, and how could she resist such an adventure with this fascinating man?

"All right," she agreed.

"Good girl. Well, we'd better get underway. It will take us a couple of hours to reach the house, and I'm sure the stew is already simmering."

The thought of the stew wasn't entirely appealing, but Cara was excited about the trip. "Shouldn't I change clothes?" she asked, looking down at her slacks and top.

"Yes," he said with a grin. "You should have on jeans and boots, but we don't have time for you to change."

Cara sensed his excitement, and it spurred her own. She was a native Californian, and until she set out to explore the country for her book, she had done very little traveling.

Unfamiliar with the areas where she had gone to research and with few connections beforehand, she hadn't had a chance to see this side of the Southern people. She had heard about the mountain heritage, and she was eager to sample a taste of it.

After they returned their horses to the stables, they climbed into Jud's car and drove off. He was a good driver, taking the curving roads with an easy mastery of the car, and Cara was able to relax and enjoy the scenery. As they began to climb into the densely wooded mountains, she understood why Jud had called this country the most beautiful God had ever created.

The road wound through a variety of trees, from pines to dogwoods, and snaked around towering mountainsides thick with lush vegetation. Cara's breath caught in her throat at some of the spectacular views down the mountainsides. Wildflowers bloomed in magnificent color along the road and carpeted the hillsides in stunning purples, reds, yellows and pinks. Flowering trees and bushes competed with each other, flaunting huge, vivid blossoms in magentas and oranges. And everywhere was the tinge of blue that cloaked the upper reaches of the mountains.

"Oh, Jud," Cara cried, gazing down at a river rushing through the trees far below them, "this really is splendid."

"I told you so, and would I lie to you?" he murmured, his gaze holding hers only briefly before it returned to the road.

"I hope not," she said quietly. He glanced at her again, and she flashed him a smile. She didn't want him to know how vulnerable she was.

Down hills and up mountains they traveled, going around bends so circuitous that Cara often held her breath. She had journeyed in Tennessee and North Carolina, and she had seen some mountains similar to these, but never had she seen such riotous beauty.

At last the road led them to the area Jud had in mind. An old log cabin was reached by climbing a red dirt road. "This must be what is known as hillbilly country," Cara commented, smiling.

"Jud laughed. "As close as you'll come to it, I promise you."

When he had parked the car, Cara listened to all the commotion from those assembled, apparently in the rear yard. "Come on," he said enthusiastically. "It sounds like half the county is here and already at the moonshine."

"Do they still drink moonshine?" Cara asked, alarmed.

He laughed softly. "Yes, as a matter of fact, some of them

do. But don't worry, you don't even have to sniff the stuff if you don't want to."

He held out his hand to her, and when Cara took it, she at once felt as if she belonged wherever he did.

"No need to bother knocking on the door," he said. "It's obvious that everyone's out back."

"I would say so," Cara agreed. Music was playing, and there were hoots of laughter and noise. When they had worked their way down the path to the people, Cara was astonished by the numbers there.

She could see why they had selected this particular house; there was a large, flat piece of land where everyone was gathered, but even at that they were crowded. A wooden platform stood in the center, and couples were square dancing under a natural canopy of shade formed by the tall trees. The hills echoed with the music of fiddles and banjos, and Cara could see that everyone was enjoying it. Most people were clapping their hands or stomping their feet to keep time to the happy beat, and Cara was enchanted by the gaiety and the light mood. She was immediately caught up in the intriguing beat and she felt her heart lighten.

"Jud," someone cried, and people began to come over. Jud introduced Cara to so many people that she couldn't possibly have kept their names straight, as he had predicted, but she took an instant liking to most of them. They were down-to-earth and warm, and she felt right at home with them.

Two mammoth iron pots filled with stew simmered over open fires, and several wooden tables were filled with mountains of fluffy white biscuits and an assortment of pies. Plastic barrels contained soft drinks and beer, and pitchers of lemonade seemed to be everywhere.

"You waited until you knew the food would be ready, didn't you?" a tall, grizzled man asked when the others had begun to drift away.

164

"Uncle Noah," Jud said warmly, turning around to greet him. "How are you?"

"I'm fine, and you, son?"

"I couldn't be better. Here," he said, ushering Cara forward, "let me introduce you to Cara Stevens."

"It's a pleasure, I'm sure, ma'am," the old man said, suddenly shy. He glanced back at Jud. "Is Justin coming?"

"I really wouldn't think so, but I didn't ask him," Jud said coolly.

"So it's still that way with you, is it?" Noah asked.

Cara noticed the tense lines around Jud's mouth, and when he didn't reply, Noah lowered his voice. "She's here, did you know?" he asked, glancing over his shoulder to where the couples were dancing.

"No, I didn't, but it doesn't matter."

His words were so sharp that Cara couldn't help but think it did matter, and her heart picked up an irregular rhythm. Surely he hadn't known that Brenda would come.

"She's married to Harrison Eanes, you know," Noah murmured.

"I heard," Jud said. At least this time his voice didn't sound so harsh, but it didn't stop Cara from experiencing a sinking feeling inside. Had Jud used her again? Surely it wasn't true.

He had thought she had some connection to Justin, so she could see how he would have benefited by making love to her if he had purposely set out to hurt his brother. But surely he didn't need to bring her, of all women, here to parade her in front of Brenda. She was sure he had no lack of female admirers, and it seemed that someone more attractive would have served his purpose better—if that was his purpose.

Involuntarily she looked around at the people, hunting for the prettiest woman. It didn't take her long to find her, and she knew without being told that the tall, buxom redhead dancing with wild abandon was Brenda. Dressed in jeans that showed off her long, slender legs and graceful hips, and a blue peasant blouse that displayed ample cleavage, she turned and spun to the lively music, the long waves of her burnished copper hair glistening in the sunlight, her blue eyes laughing enticingly. Even from where they stood, Cara could see how a man could become lost in those huge blue eyes.

When Cara looked back at Jud, she saw that his gaze had followed hers, confirming that the redhead was Brenda, but she could read nothing in his expression.

"Well, ya'll come on over and get something to drink," Noah said. "We'll be serving up the food any minute." He looked at Cara. "I hope you'll enjoy yourself."

"I'm sure I will," she murmured, but she was no longer sure at all. The excitement she had felt earlier had turned to dread, and she wondered what she was doing here. She should be home working on her book, out of harm's way.

"Would you like a soda?" Jud asked, taking her by the arm to lead her to the plastic barrels.

"Yes, I'm quite thirsty." And she was. Her mouth was so dry that she didn't think she could swallow, but it was more from nerves than thirst.

There were people standing and sitting everywhere, and though there were many chairs, most of the people had found themselves a place on the soft grass, often on a blanket. Mothers with small children had brought along playpens, and they had their babies inside.

Cara glanced at Jud; he was probably the most handsome man here. And Brenda was the prettiest woman, she thought ruefully. She simply didn't think she could bear it if he was just playing a game with her.

All her previous doubts came rushing back. Had Justin been right? No, she told herself firmly; but she wasn't sure. Why had Jud come here feeling as he did about Brenda? Or was it because he still loved her and couldn't stay away? It had appeared to Cara that he had decided on the spur of the moment to bring her here.

She couldn't ask him all the questions in her mind right now, but she could ask him some. "Jud, were you planning to come here before you took me out to the ranch and invited me?" she asked.

He looked down at her, surprise in his dark eyes. "No, why?"

"Why did you decide to come?"

"I told you. I thought you might enjoy it and I wanted you to meet some of my relatives."

It sounded so simple and so honest, and Cara wanted to believe him. She wanted to say, and what about Brenda? But she would ask later, when they were alone.

"What's wrong?" he questioned. "Are you sorry you came?"

She honestly wasn't sure. In truth, Cara had been dying to see the famous Brenda who had caused so much hurt, but now that she had seen her, she could no longer deny the depth of her own insecurity.

She was about to say she wasn't sorry when the woman herself sauntered up to them.

"Hello, Jud," she murmured warmly, her blue eyes glowing. "We didn't expect you this year."

"Oh?" he asked coolly. "And why not?"

The redhead smiled, and Cara noted that she had beautiful teeth and a truly lovely smile. "No one said anything about it." She glanced at Cara. "Aren't you going to introduce me to your friend?"

"Certainly." He put his arm around Cara's waist possessively. "This is Cara Stevens. She's a psychologist here writing a book on twins."

Cara glanced at him. Was he proud of her? Or was he merely trying to impress the woman with her label, as he called it? Surely she was jumping to conclusions, she told herself sharply. Jud Garrett didn't need to impress anyone, not even this woman.

"So you're the one," Brenda said. "I've heard about you being in town. I've also seen you on television. Somehow you look smaller in person."

Cara resisted the urge to stand up straighter. Nothing would stretch her five feet six inches, which certainly wasn't considered short but in contrast to Brenda's height did seem so.

"And slimmer, I hope," Cara joked. "I'm told the TV cameras put ten pounds on you."

"I wouldn't know," Brenda said with a warm smile. "I've never been on television."

She lingered for a moment, the silence growing between the three of them in contrast to the noise all around. "Well, I hope you two enjoy yourselves," she said at last. "It looks like the food is being served, and I'm absolutely starving."

Cara found herself thinking that even the way the woman stretched her words was appealing. Her drawl was soft and low, and her voice seductive. She could see how poor Justin could have been mesmerized by this beauty, she told herself. But how she wished that he hadn't slept with the woman. She hated the rift between the brothers, and she still hoped she could do something to heal it.

Then she found herself thinking that she never would have had the chance to know Jud intimately if he had married Brenda. If any good had come out of the dissension between the brothers, surely it was that. Or was she fooling herself again?

When she saw him watch the redhead walk away, she told herself she was going to be hurt, and hurt badly. Brenda wasn't a college homecoming queen, but she was the next best thing, and Cara was desperately afraid that Brenda still held Jud's heart in her hand.

The next two hours went by in a whirl of activity. Cara ate so much stew that she didn't think she would be able to hold another bite, but somehow she managed to eat a slice of sweet potato pie. She was even bold enough to take a swig from the moonshine jug, although she wasn't thrilled about it. She did it on a dare from Jud, and her reward was a throat on fire as the liquid burned all the way down.

"I told you I was going to have you doing things you've never done," he declared near her ear, again in that seductive way he had.

He did manage to get her up on the dance floor for some square dancing, at which she proved to be rather inept, but it didn't seem to matter as long as she had a good time. Everyone was letting his hair down, and Cara even temporarily forgot about Brenda, who eventually stretched out on a blanket beside her husband and took a nap.

Cara didn't think of her again until night had begun to fall and everyone began to gather up possessions to head home. Many of the people came over and spoke to her and Jud again, including Brenda. Cara was polite, but she noticed that Jud seemed either bored by or indifferent to the additional interest Brenda was showing in them. Was it a pretense? Or was Cara only imagining it because she wanted to think it? She had seen how irritable Jud had been when Noah mentioned Brenda.

"Time to go," Jud said, leading Cara away from the others. He squeezed her hand when they reached the car. "What did you think?" he asked.

"It was great," she replied. And it had been, in spite of Brenda being there. Cara had enjoyed herself and the others immensely.

"That was nothing," Jud murmured, nuzzling her neck as he opened the car door for her. "Now the real party begins. My cabin is just down the road."

"But aren't we going back to town?" Cara asked.

Jud shook his head. "Not on your life. We're going to my place. I want to see what you think of it."

"We can't stay long," she said firmly. "I have to get back to my book."

Jud smiled at her. "Yes, of course you do."

The way he was smiling made Cara nervous. Surely he wasn't going to try to talk her into staying the night. He wouldn't do that when he knew how close to her deadline she was. Nevertheless, the thought sent a shiver up her spine. It might be her last time with him, and if he suggested it, would she deny herself the pleasure? She wanted to tell herself yes, but somehow she didn't believe it.

CHAPTER ELEVEN

Jud's cabin was an A-frame hidden away in the dense trees less than a half-mile from where the reunion had been held. Cara could feel her heart pounding as Jud opened the car door for her.

"I hope you'll like it," he said. Night was falling fast on the mountains, but Cara was warmed by the brightness of his smile.

"It looks enchanting," she said.

"You haven't seen anything yet," he assured her, and he was right. When he unlocked the door and ushered her inside, Cara smiled. The cabin was even more welcoming than Jud's home was. A split level, with the top floor wide open and protected by only a wooden rail, the place was enchanting. The lower floor, like the living room in the house, had floor-to-ceiling bookshelves and comfortable chairs and couches. It also had a very functional kitchen–and–dining room combination.

The upper floor held a massive round bed, a stereo, throw pillows on the floor, a plush rug and a large bathroom with a Roman tub.

"It's really something," Cara murmured. "Do you get away up here often?"

"Often enough," he said with a shrug. "Sit down. Make yourself at home. I'll get us a drink."

"Fine," she murmured, but here in the intimate surroundings of his cabin she felt very vulnerable to his attractions.

Nevertheless, she meant to stick to her intention of asking him about Brenda and talking to him about his relationship with Justin. All she needed was the right moment, the right opening.

She watched as he poured whiskey into a couple of glasses, then added ice and soda for her. Her gaze was riveted on his tall, jeans-clad figure, and she resisted the urge to walk up behind him, lock her arms around his chest and lay her head on his broad back. He was so appealing, and she sensed that this night was going to be special.

When he turned around he caught her staring at him and smiled. "I hope you like what you're seeing," he said, strolling back toward her.

"Very much," she said honestly. "I find you very attractive, Jud. I won't pretend that I don't, for surely you know that already."

He settled down on the couch beside her. "And I find you beautiful," he murmured in a low, deep voice. "I have from the moment I met you." He handed her the drink. "I'm just very grateful that the attraction is mutual."

He stared at his drink for a moment, then took a swallow. His eyes settled on Cara as she took a sip of her whiskey and soda. "You're the first woman I've thought about seriously in a long, long time," he said frankly.

Cara could feel her heart beating faster. This was what she had longed to hear, had needed to hear. It was also the opening she needed to talk about Brenda and Justin.

"Brenda is very beautiful," she murmured.

Jud groaned. "Not you, too."

"What?" she asked.

"I'm sick to death of people talking to me about Brenda."

"But we need to," she said bluntly. "I saw the way you tensed when Noah mentioned that she was at the reunion."

"I tensed," he said, "because Brenda is old news. I don't want to hear about her in whispered tones for the rest of my life. What we had was over a long time ago, for God's sake."

"Listen to how angry you're getting," Cara accused, afraid that she was going to find out that he really did still love the woman.

"Don't start with the psychological analysis," he said sharply. "I don't want or need a psychologist. I never did. If you're here in that capacity, one of us has the wrong idea."

Cara was terrified that he didn't need her, period. She glanced at him with eyes darkened by doubt and pain. If he didn't still love Brenda, why wouldn't he get it out in the open? Why did he still shut Justin out?

He glared at her, and she looked back down at her drink. She should have insisted that he take her back to town after the party was over. She should have realized that she could never win in this situation.

Jud set his glass down and reached out to take her. Then he tipped her chin up with his finger and thumb. "I'm sorry I spoke so roughly to you," he said gently. "I care for you. I don't ever want to hurt you."

Cara could feel the tears building in her eyes, and she couldn't seem to stop them. She wanted this man, and not just for tonight. She wanted him with everything in her, but she always seemed to be hampered by circumstances. Time was so short. She was leaving in a matter of days. The last thing she wanted to do was fight with him. Why couldn't they get his bitter past out in the open as they had done hers and go on from there? Could they have any hope of a future as long as the past lived on within him?

With a groan he drew her to him. "Why are we always fighting about something that has nothing to do with the two of us?" he asked wearily. "I just want to love you. Is that wanting too much?"

Cara gazed into his troubled eyes. He hadn't said that he loved her. He had said that he *wanted* to love her. But that was surely enough for now, wasn't it?

She determinedly fought back her tears, but a recalcitrant dewy drop slipped down her lashes and trembled precariously there. Seeing it, Jud gently kissed it away. Then he kissed her closed lids and scattered moist kisses down her cheek until he found her mouth.

The kiss was deep and hungry, filled with a week of suppressed passion, and Cara felt her own desire mirroring his. Wasn't this time, this moment all that really mattered? She wrapped her arms around his neck and held him more tightly to her, returning all the need she found in his kiss, all the longing and wanting.

Jud's mouth moved against hers urgently as he eased her down on the plush couch cushions. Cara thrilled to the hard, lean length of him as he stretched out over her, melding to her curves. Her hands played along his muscled back, stroking and caressing, and she began to tug at his shirt, eager to feel the texture of his skin beneath her fingertips.

He moved away from her to slip his shirt from inside his pants, and then, while Cara watched, he pulled it off. When he moved back into her arms, she hungrily traced patterns on his skin, her mouth burning hotly against his.

He began to spill fiery kisses along her neck and on the sensitive skin around the neckline of her blouse. His hands found the buttons to undo them, and Cara trembled as his long, lean fingers caressed the burgeoning underside of her breasts, then circled her throbbing nipples tantalizingly. The fires were already burning inside her, sending out scorching flames, causing her hunger for this man to rage out of control. His very touch seemed to send a river of desire running in her veins.

He slipped her blouse off, and Cara locked her fingers in his hair as he began to explore her tender breasts with caressing fingers. Then he bent to lick at the taut nipples, urging them to new life, causing passion to pulse through her.

"Oh, Jud," she murmured breathlessly. "Oh, Jud." She pressed her back into the cushions and arched her body, wanting more and more of his touch.

"You feel so wonderful," he murmured thickly against her

skin, his hot breath stirring her senses further. When he began to slip her slacks down her legs, Cara closed her eyes and eagerly awaited the next onslaught of pleasure.

Jud did not disappoint her. He stroked the curves of her legs and buried deep kisses in the sensitive skin of her thighs. His touch was skilled and thrilling, and Cara reveled in it.

When he drew back from her to take off his jeans, she opened her passion-dark eyes and watched him. His gaze held hers, and she could read the desire for her burning brightly in his ebony eyes.

At last he reached for her, and to Cara's surprise, he lifted her in his arms and began to walk toward the steps. "I know just the place for this," he said thickly.

Her place, she was sure, was anywhere he was, and she kissed his mouth as he carried her upstairs. When he had taken her to the bathroom, he stood her on her feet, then turned the faucets on to fill the massive tub with water scented by wild rose petals.

As the tub was filling, he knelt in front of her and slowly, erotically, began to slip her panties down her legs. Cara trembled wildly as his hands caressed her body and his lips trailed after his fingers, stirring her soul as she had never thought possible.

"Oh, Jud," she whispered, the ecstasy becoming too much to bear without complete satisfaction.

He stood, turned off the faucets and helped her into the heavenly water. Then he sat down, stretched his legs out and eased her down on top of him. A rush of pleasure spiraled up inside her as she received him.

Cara hugged him to her, pressing her breasts against his hairy chest, her arms around his back. Jud began to kiss her again as his hips moved against hers. His hands were down low on her derrière, helping control the rhythm of their loving.

The water acted as an additional stimulant, lapping at them gently as they moved together, lost in love's most exquisite joys. Cara thought she had touched heaven when Jud claimed her before, but here in the lavish bath, her passion rose until she thought she would be lost forever in ecstasy.

"Now, Cara," Jud whispered thickly against her mouth, his breathing ragged and hoarse. "Now." Deep in the final throes of love, he arched himself against her, and they both were lost in an explosion of passion as their desire took them to love's highest peak.

For a long time after they had crested the mountains of their desire, Cara and Jud stayed in each other's arms, stroking and kissing, holding each other, enjoying the exquisite feeling of being so intimate. Then they stepped out of the water and dried each other with thick, fluffy towels.

When they were dry, Jud took Cara's hand and led her to the massive round bed. He pulled down the sheet, and Cara slipped under. After Jud had joined her he drew her to him spoon-fashion and wrapped his arms around her.

"I'm so glad you came into my life," he whispered, kissing the back of her neck where her hair lay damp. "I suppose I have Justin to thank for that."

"You do," she murmured in response, and though she knew it was a perfect time to bring up the issue of the hostility between the brothers, she was too content here in this man's arms to do anything to jeopardize the feeling. She sighed happily, snuggled down deeper in his embrace, closed her eyes and drifted into wondrous sleep.

When Cara awakened it was to the smell of bacon cooking. She looked around, then stretched, a pleased smile on her face. Last night had been so special, so precious, and she didn't want ever to leave here.

Suddenly she became wide awake. She had to get back to town and finish her book. If she took more time off, she was afraid she would hit a block and never complete the book on schedule. She glanced around the room, looking for something to put on. Spying a large closet, she went over to it to claim an oversize robe for herself.

She giggled like a young girl when she had wrapped herself in it and caught sight of her reflection in the floor-to-ceiling mirrors on the closet doors. After pushing back the baggy sleeves that completely obscured her hands, she tied the sash more tightly around her small waist, then made her way down the steps to the compact kitchen.

"Good morning," she said, walking up behind Jud as he whipped eggs in a bowl. She locked her fingers in front of him and hugged him.

"Good morning," he said, looking back over his shoulder. "I'm just getting some breakfast for us."

Cara freed him to lean against the counter, and his dark gaze flowed over her. "Anything I can do to help?" she asked, returning his grin.

"Just stand there and look pretty," he said. "Even if you are lost in that robe."

He had on a similar one, and he looked anything but lost. "Yours fits pretty well," she said, her eyes assessing the open V that revealed curling black hair.

"I hope you like it," he murmured.

"Too well, I'm afraid," she said honestly. "You're a wicked distraction, and I need to get back to town to work on my book."

He frowned. "Not right now."

Heaven knew it was the last thing Cara wanted to do, but she had responsibilities. "Not this minute, but I can't stay long."

"We have enough food to hide out here for a month," he said teasingly. "And when that runs out, we can live on love."

She didn't doubt that, and the thought sent a shiver over her skin. "It sounds quite tempting, I confess," she murmured, looking into his eyes. "But I have a deadline."

He snapped his fingers. "I know what we'll do—we'll pick up your material and you can work on the book here."

Cara laughed. "Not only would I get no work done here, but I can't possibly drag all my notes and equipment up here."

They both noticed the burning bacon at the same time, and Jud quickly picked up a fork to turn it. "See what you do to me," he said. "I get all on fire when I'm around you—and so does everything else." He shook his head. "This is ruined."

Cara smiled. "So it's on to living on love already, is it?"

Jud laughed heartily. "We could, I have no doubt, but we aren't quite down to that yet." He took more bacon out of the package and put it in the pan.

"You keep an eye on that," he said, "and I'll do the eggs." He glanced at her. "I can't be expected to think about you and cook at the same time. It's too much to ask of any man."

His words caused Cara to smile, and she made herself give her attention to the meat. Jud still hadn't spoken beyond this moment, and there was so little time left before she went back to California.

As though he could read her mind, he asked her, "When are you planning to leave for California?"

She had imagined this conversation a hundred times, but every time she had heard him saying, Don't go. Stay here with me. But he hadn't said that at all. He had merely asked her a question.

"I think I'll be finished by the end of the week." She forced herself to smile. "Unless you distract me so much that I can't do my work."

"I'll make a deal with you," he said, and Cara could feel her foolish heart beating in anticipation. "I'll leave you alone to finish your book if you'll stay an extra week here."

It wasn't quite what she had dreamed of or hoped for, but

at least he was asking her to spend more time with him. And she wanted that, even if it was all she would ever get.

"Well," she said pensively, not wanting him to know how much she desired that week with him—and how much she hoped it would mean something for their future, "I can get the book off to New York as well from here as from California."

"Good. I'm glad that's settled." He smiled at her, then went back to his cooking.

Cara had hoped he would say something more about why he wanted her to stay, and when he didn't, she sighed in resignation and turned the bacon over.

Breakfast was leisurely and should have been relaxing, but Cara couldn't seem to settle down when Jud was with her. He was exciting and stimulating, and she kept thinking that she might never see him again once she returned to California. It just didn't seem possible that he had become such an important part of her life and yet might disappear from it completely.

"I'm going out of town again on Saturday," he told her. "If you're through with the book, perhaps you'd like to go with me. I want to buy another stallion."

"Perhaps," she said. "How long will you be gone?"

"Only a day or two."

"Ask me later in the week," she said. She really wasn't sure if she would be finished, and she couldn't quit now until she was. She would stay the extra week to be with him, but she wanted it to be worry free. She didn't want to be under the pressure of her project.

"You can count on it," he said with a broad grin.

And Cara knew that she was counting on it—and the week with him—much more than she should. The thought frightened her, and she became introspective as they ate.

What would she do if Jud sent her away when the week

179

was over? How would she go on, loving him as she did? She had her plans for the future—her practice, the children she would try to help. But that future would be cold and empty without Jud.

CHAPTER TWELVE

That afternoon Cara and Jud headed back to town so that Cara could get to work. After Jud kissed her good-bye at her door, Cara watched him walk away, and she wished that she could have stayed with him at his cabin. A week without him seemed like an eternity. For the first time she resented having to spend so much time on the book. She resented anything that took her away from Jud.

A little to her surprise, he was as good as his word. Although he talked with her on the phone each day, he didn't ask to see her, and even though she wanted to see him more than she dared to admit, she kept doggedly at her work. She could see the light at the end of the tunnel, but she wasn't home free yet. The hours piled up, and then the days as she worked feverishly, always keeping in mind that she would have a whole week with Jud—even if it was the last—when she was through.

Friday came, and when Jud asked if she wanted to go with him to see the stallion he was interested in, she had to refuse. "I need just one or two more days," she told him.

"I'll put off going until you're through," he offered.

"No, why don't you go without me?" she said. She knew how eager he was to see the horse, and there was no real point in him waiting for her.

"Well, I do have an appointment with the owner," he said reluctantly.

"Go. I insist. That way I won't feel any more pressure

than I already do. There's always the possibility that I won't finish by Saturday. My last chapter is giving me a fit."

Jud laughed. "I'm convinced. But don't have a fit while I'm gone. Don't go and do anything crazy. I'm counting on that week with you more than I can say right now."

Cara could hear her own quickened breathing against the receiver, and she held it away from her mouth, hoping Jud couldn't detect it. She had already promised herself not to jump to conclusions with this man, but surely he had something extraspecial planned for their week.

"All right, Jud," she murmured breathlessly. "I'm looking forward to the week, too."

"Good," he replied before he hung up.

Cara stood looking at the phone for a long time, a smile on her lips. She would have a whole week with Jud. But she wouldn't think about that right now. She would concentrate on her book. If she thought about Jud, she *would* go crazy.

By the time Saturday afternoon came she was glad she hadn't told him she would go with him. She was in her office, still battling the wrapup of the book. So many ends had to be tied. The phone started ringing, but she was right in the middle of finally getting down on paper what had remained elusive for hours. She completed her sentence, then quickly picked up the phone, but it was too late. The party had hung up.

She sighed, then went back to her thoughts. And finally she found what she wanted. With a cry of joy she typed the last line into the computer and printed out the chapter.

Elated, she picked up her pages and purse and rushed out of the office. Suddenly she was bursting with energy. She had done it! And she felt good about the book. She wanted to celebrate, to shout, to sing. But she headed back to the apartment to await some word from Jud.

She hadn't been home more than an hour when, to her surprise, someone rapped on her door. She opened it to find

Justin standing there, dressed in a sleek black suit and white silk shirt.

"My, my, don't you look handsome," she said, smiling at him. "Where are you off to?"

"You forgot," he said in a slightly accusing tone, his dark eyes raking over her casual outfit. "You and I are going to that party tonight."

Her hands flew to her mouth. "I did forget!" she cried. "Oh, Justin, you should have phoned and reminded me."

"I tried to reach you earlier in the week but got no answer," he said. "Then I had to go out of town on a case. I just got back yesterday. I tried again today to phone but received no answer."

"Oh, dear," she murmured, opening the door wide for him. "Someone did call the office earlier, but I didn't get to the phone in time." Her gaze slid over him, and she felt terribly guilty.

"There's still plenty of time," he told her. "The party's just starting and will go on for hours. I'll wait while you get dressed."

Cara hesitated only a minute. She had promised him she would go, and she didn't want to do anything else to hurt him. "All right. You—you just make yourself at home," she said, spinning away from him.

She hadn't any idea what she would wear. He was dressed so elegantly, and most of her clothes were so casual. Abruptly she remembered the dress she had purchased to go to Jud's house, the dress she had worn the first time he tried to kiss her at the pond. She had had it cleaned, and it was lovely enough for any occasion.

Rushing off without another word, she quickly took a shower, then just as quickly dressed, catching her long hair at the nape of her neck with a fancy ivory clasp. She would have liked a more sophisticated style, but she didn't want to keep Justin waiting any longer than she had to. She felt bad enough about forgetting the party as it was.

When she had hurriedly applied a bare minimum of makeup, she returned to the living room. "Just let me call Jud's house and leave a message," she murmured.

"Jud?" Justin asked questioningly.

Smiling, Cara murmured, "I'll tell you all about it—what there is to tell—on the way to the party. By the way, where is the party?"

When he had told her, she left a message with Goldie, explaining where she would be if Jud returned and tried to reach her. Then she and Justin went out to his car.

"So, tell me," he said interestedly. "Have you honestly made some headway with that stubborn brother of mine?"

"I hope so," she answered cautiously. She met Justin's eyes. "I really do love him, Justin. He's asked me to stay a week longer." She looked away, then back at him. "I'm hoping he has a special reason for that."

Justin started the car. "You mean like proposing marriage?" he murmured incredulously.

Cara nodded. "I can dream, can't I?"

Reaching out, Justin patted her hand. "If that's what you want, I hope it comes true for you." He squeezed her fingers, then released them. "And for Jud, too. He's a lucky son of a gun, if he has sense enough to know it."

"Thank you, Justin," she murmured. "I really appreciate that."

"Sister-in-law," Justin said, trying it out. "I'd like that."

Cara laughed. "Let's not get carried away. Jud hasn't even mentioned marriage."

"Then he's a fool," Justin declared.

Cara smiled, then lapsed into thought about Jud as she and Justin made their way to the party.

It was held in a lavish home on the outskirts of town, thoroughly modern but with special charm. Cara thought that the sprawling brick structure looked regal and immensely inviting.

"Only the elite of the town get invited here," Justin murmured at her ear, smiling as the butler showed them in.

As Cara glanced around she told herself there must be at least fifty people gathered in the expansive living room. To her surprise a lovely blond woman immediately came rushing across the room to them.

Her eyes were glowing as she locked arms with Justin. "You old meanie," she murmured in a deep, throaty voice. "I've been home a week and you didn't even call."

When she noticed Cara, her cheeks colored slightly. "I'm sorry," she said politely. "I'm Susan Gibson."

Cara held out her hand. "Cara Stevens," she said warmly. "I'm pleased to meet you. I've heard about you."

"And I about you," Susan said, but there was nothing malicious in her tone. "I hope Justin hasn't been making a fool of himself over you." She sighed in an exaggerated way. "When he gets around to marrying, I'm determined to be the wife."

Cara laughed in delight at this outspoken young lady. "He wouldn't be a bad catch," she said. "I wish you all success."

"I need it," Susan said, a woeful look on her pretty face. "You have no idea. I've been dating him for four years now. You're a psychologist. Do you think the situation is hopeless?"

"Ladies, if you don't mind," Justin broke in, his voice long suffering. "I am alive and well, and I hear every word you're saying. Let's not talk as if I'm not even here." He glanced from one to the other. "I would have made the introductions if you had only waited."

"Women's lib," Susan said playfully. "We can do it ourselves."

"There is such a thing as good manners," Justin said in a mock-stern tone, and Cara was immediately reminded of Jud and the night he had come looking for her when she had rudely gone off to the pond without telling anyone.

A small band began to play an old-fashioned waltz, and a

very distinguished gentleman came and held out his arm to Susan. "Excuse us," she said, and she vanished into the crowd as quickly as she had appeared.

"Who was that mysterious lady?" Cara demanded, her tone only a little teasing. "You *are* an old meanie, Justin. Why were you making advances to me when you've obviously been stringing that girl along for years?"

Justin looked a little sheepish as he held his arms out to her. "Dance with me and I'll tell you."

"How can I resist?" she murmured with a laugh. She really was curious to hear his explanation.

He began to guide her gracefully around the dance floor. "Well?" Cara prompted.

"I'm working on it," he replied. "I'm trying to decide where to begin." He glanced across the room at Susan. "She was my girl when I made love to Brenda," he said tiredly. "I think the whole damned town must have heard about that little to-do because of the split between Jud and me. I didn't talk, and Jud didn't, but it leaked out anyway—perhaps from Brenda when Jud dumped her. Anyway, to make a long story short, I broke up with Susan. She asked for an explanation, and I gave one. Oddly, she forgave me."

He was looking at Cara, but he seemed to see right through her. "I just haven't forgiven myself."

"I can see that," she murmured, "but that still doesn't explain the situation to me. Susan seems like such a delightful girl. Why haven't you married her? Why are you running around romancing strangers like me? What if I had fallen for you?"

Justin sighed. "You won't believe this, but I honestly think I keep chasing women so that I *won't* marry Susan." He looked away again, and Cara could see color climbing up his neck. "I don't think I have a right to marry and be happy when I'm the reason Jud never married, the reason he's so bitter about women."

"Oh, Justin," Cara murmured compassionately, "don't do

that to yourself. You've tried to make amends for your mistake. Don't pay your whole life for it. Good Lord, man, don't make Susan pay for it. She must love you, though heaven only knows how she endures your playing around."

For the first time since they had started dancing, Cara saw Justin's familiar smile. "I think I'm going to like having a psychologist in the family." He winked at her. "You get Jud married and that leaves me free and clear to do the same."

"Justin," she cried, her voice full of alarm, "please don't wait for that! Don't let him rule your life like that."

Moved by her distress, Justin leaned down and lightly brushed her lips. "Thanks for making me finally wake up. You know I never honestly thought about why I hadn't married Susan. She really *doesn't* deserve that treatment."

They were so absorbed in the conversation that neither Cara nor Justin saw Jud walk up behind them. She spun out of Justin's arms when she saw his eyes widen in surprise. At the same time she felt the bite of Jud's fingers on her bare shoulder.

"I'd like to talk to you," he said sharply, his voice low and harsh.

"Fine," she replied.

Cara could feel his anger pulsing through his very fingers, and when she looked back at Justin, she saw that he was concerned for her.

"If you'll excuse us, Justin."

He started to protest, but when Cara frowned at him, the words died on his lips.

His hand tightly gripping her arm, Jud led Cara out through wide doors to a flower garden in the back of the house.

"So," he said once they were out of hearing of the others, "you couldn't go with me, but that certainly doesn't stop you from turning up here with Justin. You weren't too busy with your book to spend time with him. Justin, of all people! What do you think you're doing?"

187

Cara could feel the anger rising all the way from the tips of her toes, gaining momentum as it rushed up her body.

"Enough!" she cried. "Enough of this crazy jealousy where Justin is concerned. I'll tell you what I'm doing." Her voice was rising, but she didn't care. "I'm at a party with your brother, dancing with him, because I promised him I would come. I had forgotten all about it. I just finished my book this afternoon, and since you were out of town anyway, I decided to keep my promise to Justin."

"And what prompted you to let him kiss you in front of all those people? What explanation do you have for that?"

Now Cara's rage exploded. "That's it, isn't it?" she cried. "Your brother and me making love in front of all those people—just like Justin and Brenda! Oh, Jud, when will you let go of the past? When will you thank Justin for saving you from a woman like Brenda? You should count your blessings for what happened—and that it happened before you married her."

Jud's anger was just as out of control as Cara's. "I did thank my lucky stars that I found out what kind of woman she was, but I didn't want to learn it from my own brother," he said harshly.

"And do you know why that hurt you so much, Jud?" she demanded. "Do you know why you can't forgive him?" She didn't wait for him to answer. "Because you loved him so much—much more than you loved Brenda—because of the twin bond, because he was like a part of you, and his betrayal was too painful to accept."

"That's not it," Jud growled.

"It is," Cara retorted. "And you know it is. You still love him, Jud. But your pride won't let you forgive him now. If you didn't love him you wouldn't have stayed right here in this same town with him, enduring a situation that most of the town knew about."

"No," he denied violently. "No, that's not true."

"It *is* true!" she declared. Then, abruptly, her anger

188

seemed to run its course. She couldn't battle this man here at a stranger's house. Besides, he would never listen. She was wasting her time. He was so bitter that he couldn't see the forest for the trees, and until he resolved the primary relationship in his life, Cara couldn't hope that he could have a satisfactory one with her. He was consumed by his hatred of Justin. It warped all his other feelings.

"I'm sorry for you, Jud," she murmured. "And for me." Then she turned on her heel and hurried away before he could see her tears start to fall.

For a long time Jud stared after her, absorbing her words. Every single thing she had said was true—every word of it. He had known it himself for far too long, but he hadn't been able to admit it. It *was* time he put his bitter past behind him, past time. He just hadn't had a strong enough reason until Cara came into his life. And now that he did have a reason, what was he going to do about it?

Cara was in her apartment packing when she heard a car pull up outside. Her fingers paused, trembling over the garment she had just laid in the suitcase. She heard someone slam a car door, then walk up the steps to her rooms. The knock on the wood went right through her heart, and for a moment she stood there, her eyes closed, not daring to look. Was it Jud? Had he decided to listen to her after all? Or was it Justin, wondering where she had gone?

On shaking legs she made her way across the room to the door. When she opened it, she found Jud standing before her. She wanted to rush into his arms and weep in relief, but it was too soon. He hadn't said a word. She didn't know what he would say.

He cleared his throat. "May I come in?"

"Yes." She backed away so that he could enter. She was sure the anxiety she was experiencing would kill her as she waited for him to speak.

He closed the door behind him. For the first time since

Cara had known him, she saw that he was at a loss for words. His dark eyes held hers, and she waited.

"This isn't easy for me," he said in a thick voice. "I'm here first of all because I lied when I told you last Sunday that I didn't need you. I do. As a woman and as a psychologist, too, it seems."

He looked away, and Cara desperately wished there were some way to make this easier for him, but he had to say it, to admit it to himself and to her. He stood before her, rigid and full of pride.

"You were right. As twins, Justin and I were closer than most brothers. Justin knew me better than anyone."

He gazed back into her eyes. "It is true that he tried hard all his life to excell because he was the second son, but it never became a personal competition between us. We always understood each other so well."

He paused, and Cara nodded sympathetically but did not interrupt. She knew he had to do this in his own way.

"When I found Brenda I thought I had discovered the perfect woman. Apparently Justin agreed."

Cara felt tears welling up in her eyes, and she blinked. Jud's pain was her pain. She loved him. She hated to see him hurt, but he needed to purge himself of his bitter memories.

"I submerged my feelings for Justin beneath my bitterness," Jud murmured. "Time passed, and as time will, it eased the ache and the memories." He sighed. "But there just never seemed to be any way to bridge the gap between us, even though I realized eventually that I was well rid of Brenda."

His ebony eyes held hers. "Then you started calling. I didn't want you prying and poking, discovering what had happened between my brother and me. But I began to see it as a possible way to mend broken fences."

"Is that why you finally agreed to talk to me?" Cara asked.

190

Jud nodded. "I invited you both to the house, thinking maybe Justin and I could finally solve our problems."

He reached out and traced her cheek with his fingertips. "Then I saw you, and that very first time I felt an attraction I'd never felt for another woman. I thought you were seeing Justin, but that didn't stop me from wanting you. It brought back all the old feelings, and I was so shocked by that realization that I couldn't speak to Justin then."

"But surely later . . ." Cara suggested.

Jud looked away. "The longer I waited, the more difficult it became to break that long silence." He paused, then added, "But I finally did it tonight. After you left the party, Justin and I had a long talk. I think we've both finally managed to forget the past."

"Oh, Jud," she whispered, sliding her arms around his waist.

He held her to his body. "I didn't trust you. At first you wouldn't tell me if you were involved with Justin, and I wondered if you were another Brenda who found making love with twins appealing."

He tilted her chin and looked into her eyes. "And when I fell in love with you, I was doubly ashamed of my attitude toward my brother all these years. But I still wouldn't admit to myself what the problem was. And you—you kept telling me how much alike the two of us were, so alike. I wanted to deny everything you said because the memories and the realities were too painful.

"I've been very stubborn, but I love you, Cara. Next week, when you were finished with your book and we could spend time concentrating on just the two of us, I planned to ask you to marry me."

For the first time a hint of a smile played on his beautiful lips. "Besides, I felt I had to keep you with me. I couldn't possibly let a woman like you escape—a woman who knows more about me than I do myself. It could be dangerous."

Cara smiled. "I don't want to escape. I never did." She

leaned away from him a little. "And I was so afraid you were going to let me go anyway. I love you, Jud. You've taught me what the word really means."

He groaned as he drew her against him. "I want to teach you even more. I want you. I want you to live your life here with me. Will you marry me?"

Cara paused cautiously before she gave in completely to her heart. "What about my career? I love you, but I won't give up everything I've worked for."

"And I wouldn't ask you to," he replied. "I know how much your work means to you. You can open a practice here as well as elsewhere. I want you to be happy. What do you say?"

"Yes," she cried. She knew it would be a good marriage because they had already learned so much from each other: She had taught him to face the past, and he had taught her to face the future.

His head lowered, and he claimed her mouth in a passionate caress. Cara wrapped her arms around his neck and returned his kiss, sealing the promise of a future of love, the beginning of an exciting voyage of togetherness.